desecrated ESSENCE

For all Content Inquiries, please visit my website:
CONTENT WARNING | www.careneauthor.com

Please read responsibly.

PLAYLIST

Chase Atlantic - Church

Marilyn Manson - Tourniquet

Halestorm-I miss the misery

Halestorm-I get off

The pretty reckless- my medicine

Christina Perri - Jar of Hearts

Bishop Briggs - Dark Side

Chase Atlantic - Right Here

Motionless in White - Another Life

Weeknd – Often

Corpse – Miss You

Door Number Two – Every Damn Day

JC Stewart – I Need You to Hate Me

DEDICATION

Only time has the complete power to heal and unfortunately, some of us just don't have enough of it. Make use of the time you're given.

Before you know it… It's taken away.

BRODY

PROLOGUE

I watch her letting him guide her with his hand on her lower back, and let a growl escape my lips. Doesn't she wonder where I am? After everything we've been through, she's still treating me like I'm nothing. This fucker, The Teacher, is helping her into his vehicle, and she looks up at him with a laugh. Her eyes squint, and I just know the hazel is shining brightly in them, like they once did for me. I want to rip that laugh out of her throat and ram it down his. Their relationship is the hardest to watch, and that's all I've been doing… Watching.

When it's Cooper, they're playful and annoyingly content. With Caine, it's intense and borderline dangerous. But with this one, she feels protected and secure. I hate this one the most, not that I don't hate the others, but this one leaves me burning to maim.

He leans into the passenger seat, pressing his lips into

hers, and I can imagine she moans like the wanton whore she's become.

He's made it a habit to park his car a few blocks from the school so as not to attract attention, but I see them.

I always see them.

They drive off, and I lean back against the brick, fighting with the monster within. The one that wants to watch her suffer at its hands because she killed my brother, because she loves *them*, because she fucking left me. I'm constantly at war with him, but he's starting to make me see his perspective. She needs to pay for her wrongs.

Everyone pays eventually. I stare down at my hands, still tinged in pink, and scrape some dry, rust-colored blood from under my nails.

Everyone will pay.

KAILEY HIMARI

ONE

Brody has been missing for three months. *Three months!* The guys have searched and concluded that he'll come back when he's ready. I can't believe they aren't worried. I'm worried and I know he and I are as far on the outs as we can get. Georgina has also been missing for three months… Knowing they're together only makes my hatred for her burn hotter. He still wants her after everything she's done. His inner turmoil calls to her toxicity like a moth to the flame.

I've watched it with familiarity since we were thirteen years old. How her eyes follow him, and his body automatically curls toward hers when she's nearby. Jealousy is an emotion I've let control me for so long. I've been jealous of her, jealous of the golden four, and jealous of just about any girl who giggles at the attention of a boy.

Brody wasn't here when his family buried Justin—car accident is their story—and again when Lance's family buried him. Nor has his family released any information about their son's disappearance. Everyone just assumes he'll be back. I can't help but wonder… Will he be back?

The last three months for me have been a whirlwind. Oliver found my papa in the bayou, in a well-known crack house, and blitzed out of his fucking mind. He's been in a rehab facility for the past ninety days and will continue to stay there for another thirty. When I found out he was abusing drugs and alcohol, it felt like a punch to the gut.

All the warning signs were there, but I failed to see them. I was so engrossed in my own problems that I didn't see my only family left needed me. The guilt I carry with me could knock me down. I don't let it; I keep going day-by-day and hope one day it's not the first thing I think about when I wake up.

The only things that keep me from completely crumbling are my boys. Yeah, it's weird. I have *boyfriends*, y'all.

They have been helping me keep things afloat. With my pa gone and the dealership closed, I've had to find a job to keep up with some bills, and the guys have helped with everything else. Mortgage, credit card debt, and keeping my fucking lights on. They're also paying for my papa's treatment.

Even Zeke has been coming around to check up on me. He installed a new security system in my house so I would feel safer when I'm here alone, which is rare. There's always one of them here.

Like right now, in fact, Zeke is sitting on my worn leather couch with me as we play the newest GTA video game. It was a smooth transition back into our old friendship, and we haven't looked back.

I haven't seen Faith around, but I know they are still together. I've heard the others speak about it. He doesn't talk much about her, but I see her name flash on his phone often. Again, the jealousy burns molten when I think of them together, and I let it burn like an old friend you just can't let go of, no matter how awful they are for you.

"Where's my hot piece of ass?" Caine's deep rumble has me breaking my concentration with the game. I watch helplessly as my car veers into a brick wall.

"Look what you did," I pout at him and squeal when he jumps on top of me.

"Well, I guess we're done for the day, bebelle," Zeke chuckles and gets up.

Before I can respond, Caine has my chin in a deadlock, and my mouth thoroughly devoured. The noises I'm making can't be helped, and my legs fall open to give him easier access to where I want him.

I hear Zeke clear his throat. "I'll see y'all later then."

Caine breaks our kiss and looks at Zeke over his shoulder. "You can always stay and watch." He punctuates his point by driving his hips into mine.

Again, I can't even control the mewling noise that leaves my throat at the feel of his large cock pressing into my center.

Zeke's eyes meet mine over Caine's shoulder, and I bite my lip as I see the lust in his.

I want him to watch. I want his eyes to rove over me with a hunger he can't wait to satiate.

He shakes his head and leaves the room in a hurry.

"His loss," Caine growls just before he drags my leggings down.

I don't have much time to prepare as his mouth latches onto my clit and his tongue lashes against it. I dig my fingers into his short, cropped hair and push his face in closer. Caine is like a hurricane; he forces his way in and leaves you feeling broken when he's done. In his defense, he always warns me ahead of time.

"Put your hands over your head and don't bring them down," he demands, and I feel the rush of wetness at his words.

He grabs my thighs in his hands and spreads me further. He's staring down into my pink folds as I move my hips in anticipation.

"Kailey," he warns me, giving me a look that says he wants to punish me.

Fuck it, I want him to punish me too.

I wiggle my hips again and nearly come when I hear him growl. With no other warning, he flips me around and props my ass high in the air. I feel his teeth first as he bites down on my right ass cheek, but it's the slap on the left that startles me. I cry out at the sting of both assaults, then moan as the sensations spread over me.

"Did someone get herself in trouble?" I hear Cooper's drawl from the doorway.

"Get over here and fill her mouth with something while I redden her ass," Caine orders him.

Cooper, ever the willing participant, has his pants dropped, then sits beside me on the couch. From the look of the tent he's sporting, he's ready to go.

"Kailey." Caine grabs my hair and lifts me up. "I want to hear you gag on him. Am I clear?"

I want to. My mouth is watering, and my eyes don't leave Cooper's as I lick my lips, but I guess Caine was waiting for my answer. His grip on my hair tightens as he pulls me up roughly so my back hits his front.

"Is there any particular reason why you haven't answered me yet?" His voice is low and dark. So very fucking dark.

"Sorry," I whisper. "The answer is yes."

"Good girl." His breath washes over my cheek, and I moan in the aftermath of his gratification.

Yeah, it's messed up that I want this after everything I've been through, but I don't give a fuck. I like it. No, I fucking love it.

He pushes me back down, and my face lands roughly in Cooper's lap. I grab the waistband of his boxers and pull them down. When his dick springs out, my mouth salivates. I want him so badly.

"I want to hear those gags," Caine reminds me as I hear the clink of his belt coming undone.

Just the thought of being between the two of them used to throw me into an episode where I would be catatonic. But now… It's something I look forward to. Caine and Cooper have rewired my brain, and I no longer fear the feel of two men against me.

I lick the tip of Cooper's cock and taste his salty pre-cum. I love the feel and taste of him. I open my mouth and begin to slowly work my way down his length, bobbing my head to a rhythm I know he likes.

He curses under his breath and runs his fingers along my cheek. Where Caine is all rough and hard edges, Cooper is sweet and soft. The perfect balance.

I feel my legs being spread wider, then the head of Caine's huge cock pushing its way inside me. The initial stretch always hurts, no matter how prepared I am.

His hand grips into my hair, and he pushes me down

farther onto Cooper's cock, forcing me to gag. Cooper moans around my throat's constriction as I struggle to relax.

"I told you to gag on it," Caine grunts, then slams himself all the way inside me.

The motion causes me to take Cooper even farther down my throat, and I'm gagging once again.

"That's it," Caine encourages. "Let me hear how badly you want to breathe."

Then he's lifting my head and groaning as I audibly suck in air. He begins a punishing rhythm, and my moans are becoming louder. His hand slaps down onto my right cheek and then once again to the left. I don't know how I ever lived without them.

"Suck his dick, then I want to hear you slurp his cum."

His words have me clenching around his girth, and the sound of my arousal grows louder throughout the room.

I do as he asks, taking Cooper back into my mouth. With each of Caine's forceful thrusts, Cooper's cock hits the back of my throat. I reach my hand out and massage his balls, his cock jerking in response.

"Sha." Cooper's voice is husky and filled with lust. "I'm going to..."

I feel his cock jerk, and moan with my approval as the first squirt of his cum hits my tongue.

"Slurp," Caine growls, and I do as he asks.

I slurp Cooper's cock like a melting popsicle on a hot summer day, the noise of my sucking and smacking lips spurring Caine on. I feel the gathering sensation in the bottom of my stomach, and it slowly spreads down my legs and up my torso. I clench Caine's dick and scream his name as I explode around him.

"Fuck," Cooper groans. "I will never get enough of that."

Caine pulls me up, so my back is once again against his front, and his mouth fuses to my neck. He hasn't broken his rhythm yet, and I scream when his teeth clamp down on my skin. This is his favorite way of branding me and making me his. I have teeth marks all over my body.

His strokes become erratic, and I know he's on the edge. I reach behind us both and grab his ass cheek, giving him a hard squeeze. He growls into my neck and pumps into me once more before spilling his load.

"Fuck," he says through clenched teeth. "Why is this pussy so good?"

"I love you too," I say as I fall forward into Cooper's arms.

Cooper plays with my hair as Caine goes to grab a towel. Again, this is our routine aftercare, same shit each time. Caine is rough, and Cooper is sweet. He brings me comfort after I've been thoroughly ravished by Caine.

Caine carefully cleans me up and brings me my leggings. Then he pulls me up and gathers me in his lap on the couch. He smells like me and something I could only describe as home.

"I love you," he whispers in my ear, and I smile.

"Sha, I actually came here to talk to you about something." Copper chuckles, then reaches out to twist some of my hair around his finger. "Not that I'm complaining."

I feel Caine's chest moving as he laughs softly.

"What is it?" I ask him.

"Casey called me last night." I sit up at those words and

can't help the jealousy that invades my senses.

"For what?" I don't even sound like myself.

"Hold on." He raises his hands. "Not for anything like that." His mouth is turned up into a mischievous grin.

I know I really don't have a right to feel this way. I'm currently in love with three different guys, but shit, they were the ones to set this up.

"Spit it out," I say with a huff.

"She hasn't heard from Georgina since she disappeared with Brody."

"And?" I roll my eyes.

"That's strange," Caine rumbles from underneath me. "Georgina likes to brag about all the extravagant things in her life. She'd be bragging her ass off if Brody took her somewhere for this long."

"Have they ever been away for this long?" I ask them.

"Sometimes they would go for summer break and come back to school later, but to be honest, this isn't the best time for Brody to disappear," Caine answers me.

"Why?"

"We have a lot going on right now," Cooper's answer is evasive, and I decide not to push him for more.

"So what are you thinking?" I look between them.

"I'm thinking we need to find Brody. I don't think he took Justin's death too well," Cooper mutters.

"I don't even care," Caine growls. "I don't regret a single thing."

I stand up and pace the room. "What about Zeke? He

and Brody seem tight. Does he know anything?"

"Zeke has been weirdly tight-lipped." Cooper looks at Caine.

"Yeah, I think he knows more than he's saying. I haven't really pressed him because he's our brother, but I think it's time we do." Caine nods.

"You talk to him," Cooper says and stands. "I'll stay with Kailey."

"Sounds good." Caine stands and pulls me into his arms. "I'll be back later."

His hand grips my ass cheek roughly and his teeth clamp down on my bottom lip. I feel the sting, then taste the rusty hints of blood. He sucks my lip into his mouth and moans when he tastes it too.

"Fucking delicious," he says as he pulls away.

Then I watch as he leaves the room in long, quick strides. So fucking destructive, but so fucking hot.

"I never thought I'd see the day he'd fall in love." Cooper snickers. "I was sure every girl would run from him, except for you. I knew you would be perfect."

"Yeah, I don't know how you saw that. Maybe one day you can explain it."

His chin drops to his chest as he watches me in a devious way. I squeal when he stalks forward. Before I can move, he has me over his shoulder and makes his way to my room.

I guess that blowjob just wasn't enough.

BRODY

TWO

I watch as Caine leaves her house with a small smile on his face, like he knows a secret no one else has figured out. Fuck him… I created that fucking secret. The girl in this house is the way she is because of me, and watching these fuckers claim her makes me want to watch them bleed.

Cooper is still in there, and I clench my teeth as I think about exactly what they're doing right now. I wonder if she imagines my cock inside her, making her moan, and making her come so hard. I need to see if he can make her come as hard as I know I could.

Getting into Kailey's house was never hard. I had this shit down when I was ten years old. Her parents' bedroom window never locks right, and if you jimmy it just right, it slips open no problem. It is on the second floor, but they have a balcony up there that just so happens to hang conveniently beside the fence.

I climb the fence, grab the balcony to pull myself up, then voila! I'm in front of the window. Yeah, the balcony door locks tight, but the window is fucked, and her father never thought it was an issue. It's a fucking issue because I make sure I pay her a visit at least once a week… For the past four years.

The window opens, and I pull myself inside. I hear Kailey's squeal, and then one set of pounding footsteps coming up the stairs. I don't bother to hide myself as Cooper rushes by with Kailey thrown over his shoulder. They never pay attention to their surroundings, and it'll be something I will talk to all of them about when I get back.

I step out of her father's room and walk across the hall to her room. This time, they didn't even bother to close the door. Outside, the last of the sun's rays are shining oranges and reds across the sky and the natural light is slowly dimming. The shadows I've become so accustomed to are slowly closing in around me.

Cooper throws her down onto the bed, and I watch as her body bounces once before settling into her plush blanket. Kailey has changed over the last four years. Her hair is darker, her face is sadder, and her body is filled out in all the right places. Places begging to be touched, places Cooper has his hands on right now, and it makes my blood pound through my chest.

He pulls her shirt off, and her breasts are pushed high by her black, lace push-up bra. Kailey's stomach is toned, and her skin is this olive complexion that borders on creamy. She has one beauty mark under her left breast, sitting right on top of her ribs, and her collarbones cast shadows on her chest that scream to be ravished.

Cooper quickly pulls off her leggings, and I almost snort out loud. He never was a patient lover. If I were him right now, I'd be tasting her skin, dipping my tongue in all her crevices, running my fingertips over her soft lips, and breathing in her essence.

She's just as frantic, ripping his shirt up over his head and pushing his pants down with her toes curled into the waistband. It's like watching a pair of virgins fumble about, and it makes me angry all over again. Kailey once wanted me to be her first, I could see it in the way she watched me. She wore her heart on her sleeve, and I couldn't ignore the feelings she had when she constantly smothered me with them. It was confusing because Kailey was my safe haven, sharing her family with me and her home, while I struggled to figure out why I couldn't feel *anything*. I was protective of her, almost violently so, and there was nothing I wouldn't do for her at one time, but was that love? I don't know.

It all changed the day her mother died, and Kailey threw me aside like trash, taking all my feelings for her with it.

Cooper's fingers run through her glistening folds, and it takes everything in me not to storm in there and show him how to properly touch a girl. I would open her thighs slowly, biting my way up from her knee, savoring the feel of her skin between my teeth, testing her pain threshold as I made my way to her pussy. Judging by the bite marks all over her skin, Caine already knows where her threshold stands, and it makes me want to sink a knife into his neck.

Cooper pulls her bra down, doesn't even take the time to slowly reveal her dusty rose nipples before latching his mouth to one. Her back arches as she moans, and I can't help but feel like I could make her do that louder.

Cooper's hard cock bumps against her pussy, and she pants as she lifts her waist, trying to put him exactly where she wants him. I hate how she wants him this much, wants his cock inside of her, and acting so fucking frenzied for it.

His mouth fuses to hers in a sloppy kiss as he grabs his cock and lines it up with her pussy. He's not wearing a condom? He's just pushing his way into her with nothing? He thinks he's worthy to feel her completely with no barriers? And she's fine with it?

His cock slams in to the hilt, and I curl my hands into fists to stop myself from storming in there. The monster inside bristles and stretches awake as he senses my overwhelming need to kill someone.

Cooper slowly pulls out, and I see her arousal gleaming on the smooth skin of his cock. She's so fucking wet for him, and the rise in anger causes the monster inside to scratch at my skin. He wants to sink his claws into them both and watch as they struggle to hold on to the last vestiges of life.

Cooper begins a steady rhythm of pulling out slowly and slamming back into her. She has her head tipped back as she lets out loud moans of satisfaction, and I force myself to watch even though her neck is calling to me. A neck with prominent teeth marks marring the perfect skin, a neck I can easily wrap my hand around, then enjoy watching her struggle to breathe.

The scent of them fucking reaches me, and my nostrils flare at the heady assault. I can't stay here and watch them come. I can't do it and keep myself together. It would be impossible. His cum shooting inside her without obstruction and desecrating her very essence. Fuck watching that.

Turning on my heel and taking deep calming breaths, I leave their moans and groans behind me. I could go back out the way I came in, but I rarely do that. As easy as it is to climb up, it's a lot harder to climb down, and besides, I like the twinge of excitement when I think about getting caught.

I head down the stairs and turn left into the kitchen. It's dark, but I see The Teacher's coat hanging on the chair. He practically lives here now, and his scent is fucking everywhere. He must be here somewhere, and I bet he's outside waiting until they finish upstairs. Fucking pussy.

I know who he is and what family he comes from. The

Ballon mob is a large, corrupted organization that gives my father's organization a run for their money… Literally. I know his two older brothers are gifted in the murder department. Their expertise is almost like a work of art, but Oliver Ballon ran away from home when his father forced him to take his first life. Probably cried like a baby and then tucked his balls up into his stomach to become a *guidance counselor.*

I peer out the door into the backyard, and just like I thought, *Mr. Ballon* is standing in the center of the yard looking at the purple Wisteria tree. I wonder how he's feeling right now, knowing another cock is balls deep in the woman he loves. Does he feel anger like me? Does he look at Caine or Cooper and feel the indescribable need to murder them? It's in his blood, after all… Murder.

Maybe not. Like I said, he tucked his balls up a long time ago. Maybe he's just standing out there looking at some fucking flowers, like the little pussy he is. Well, he's fucking up my escape plan because now I have to wait until he comes back inside.

I grab the last apple from the bowl on the table and crunch into its green skin, the sour juice dribbling down my chin. It takes a whole five minutes for the guy to come back inside. By this time, I've already finished the apple and placed the core back into the bowl. I stand to the side, watching as he strolls to the base of the stairs and stares up toward the bedrooms, his hand rubbing along the base of his neck.

Maybe she's fucking three guys to compensate for the fact that not one of them is an actual man.

KAILEY HIMARI

desecrated ESSENCE

THREE

Oliver is standing in my doorway when I get out of the shower. He's talking to Cooper about something quietly as he lies on my bed with just his boxers on. It's no secret I'm sleeping with all three of them, but it's still awkward when it's blatant in the others' faces.

"Hey." I smile at Oliver as I walk over to kiss him.

He smells like his cologne and bourbon. Lately, Oliver has been drinking more, and the thought scares me because of the situation with my papa. I know it's not the same, but I worry, nonetheless.

"Let's go get something to eat." I head into my closet, quickly dressing in an oversized hoodie and leggings.

Oliver and I head downstairs while Cooper hops in the shower. Cooper and I have been connecting a lot lately with our sexual appetites. I don't know what it is about him, but whenever we find ourselves alone, we just can't keep our hands off each other. We're always in a hurry to feel our skin touch and to become connected in the most intimate way possible.

The backdoor is sitting slightly open, and I stop to frown at it.

"Why is that open?" My heart speeds up, and I feel myself slipping. It's been months since my last episode, but I will never forget what it feels like when it starts its onslaught.

"Must have been me." Oliver goes to the door and closes it. "I was out there earlier."

I try to calm down at his words, but it takes a while to relax. I don't think this feeling will ever completely leave me. I will always be damaged by what happened.

"Kail?" His hands softly touch my face, and I will myself to stay here in the present. His touch is not theirs. Caine and Cooper killed them; they can never do what they did to me to anyone ever again.

"Sorry," I murmur when I finally bring myself around. "I can't seem to let it go."

"Let it go?" He gathers me in his arms. "You will never be expected to let it go. You've come so far. I'm proud of you."

His words always have a calming effect on me. He knows exactly how to build me up when I feel like I'm sinking fast.

"What do you feel like eating?" I make my way to the fridge.

An apple core is sitting in a fruit bowl on a table, making me pause mid-stride. I'm not throwing this one out. I will make Cooper do it himself.

I open the fridge and start pulling out the ingredients to make an omelet. "Eggs?" I look at Oliver with a smile.

"Sure." He grins, and moves around, gathering everything we need.

"That smells good." Cooper inhales soundly when he walks into the kitchen.

"You're not getting anything if you can't start cleaning up after yourself." I give him my sternest look.

"Sha, what are you talking about?"

"The apple cores you keep leaving in my fruit bowl. That's like the second one this week." I point at the table.

He has a look of confusion on his face as he follows my finger. I don't like it, and it sets my blood pounding once again.

"I hate apples." He shrugs. "Unless it's in pies."

"Oliver?" I know it's not him. He is meticulous in his cleanliness.

He shakes his head and goes to the apple to pick it up.

"Maybe Caine," Cooper says, but he doesn't look convinced. I've never seen Caine eat anything other than his lean meats and veggies, or a protein shake.

"Or Zeke." Oliver shrugs, then tosses the core into the garbage.

"If it was Zeke, that core would've been completely brown." I can feel the tremors starting in my hands.

"Sha." Cooper places his hands on my shoulders. "Don't panic. They're gone," he says the last part in a whisper.

I know they're gone, and Georgina is out there somewhere with that information with Brody. Brody... Who said he would kill me, and then devoured my mouth before disappearing.

"Relax," Oliver soothes. "We'll figure it out."

What they don't know is how the nightmares still plague me, and sleeping has become somewhat of a chore. My attacks have lessened, but I still get random bouts of anxiety.

My phone pings beside me, and I see my best friend's name flash across the screen. She's also been my sunshine on the darkest of days.

Kimmy: Boo! Tomorrow is the last day before the holiday break. What are we doing?

I can feel her excitement bleeding through her words.

Me: This holiday I will be with Cooper's family for Christmas, but we have absolutely no idea for New Year's.

Kimmy: Yes! I'm on it!

"Looks like we'll be having New Year's with Kimmy and Henry," I tell Oliver and Cooper.

"Finally." Cooper exhales. "I want to pick that guy's brain about the Wave's team."

"I haven't celebrated a New Year in a long time," Oliver says as he comes to stand behind me.

"This year I will kiss the three best things to ever happen to me." I grin at him from over my shoulder.

"This year I will have something worth celebrating." His reply melts my heart.

"This year I propose we go out with a bang… Literally," Cooper cuts in. "All fucking four of us. You think you could handle that, sha?"

I let the words hit me and wait for the telltale rush of an anxiety attack. Instead, I find my panties a little moist.

ZEKE

FOUR

I don't know what's happening to me. I'm happy to be back in Kailey's orbit—that's what it feels like—but with it comes a lot of confusion. She's dating two of my boys and a guidance counselor, but here I am thinking of what her kisses might taste like.

I think it's because of all the time we're spending together, and I feel propelled back in time to when she was all I saw. Back when we were kids, Kailey was more than just my best friend, she dominated all my thoughts. Even after the last few hours with Faith, I'm leaving her house with Kailey still on my mind.

"That pussy is becoming routine now?" Brody's dark voice hits me from the shadows of Faith's house.

"I told you to keep a low profile," I snarl at him. "Did anyone see you?"

"No." He shrugs, then grins… Fucking psycho. "I paid a visit to our boys. They are too wrapped up in a chick's pussy to get any work done."

"You were in her house again? Bro, that's not keeping a low profile." I tip my head back.

"Speaking of, I need you to say you ate apples."

"I ate apples?" I look at him like he's lost it. Actually, I know he has. "Tell me you're taking your meds."

"I ate a few apples at Kails'. Just say it was you," he huffs.

"Fuck," I growl. "You need to come back now. We have a lot of shit to get done."

"I've already fucked my father over. His clients are done and no one trusts him now. I've derailed every shipment."

"I know." I scrub my hand down my face. "But the rest of us need you."

"I've referred a new member to Caine and helped him win a new contract his father was scouting. I've sent Cooper a lead on a company looking for a bid better than his father's, and I handed you a firm to work with on a silver platter, all while I've been gone." He does air quotes for 'gone'.

"The guys don't know that it came from you. To them, you're out doing whatever while we scramble to work our shit out." He looks at me like he couldn't care less, and I guess that's probably true. "How much longer?"

"I'm almost done. Give me three weeks… Tops."

"That's the entire holiday break," I say, exasperated.

"Oui, I'll be back in time for the last semester." He grins at me again.

"Take your meds," I tell him as I walk toward my motorcycle.

"Don't get sucked in by her pussy," he calls out to me. "She's already got three others in there."

"Fuck me," I mutter, then get on my bike.

Brody has been in a steady downfall since the beginning of high school. His household is filled with hatred and contention, his relationship with Georgina is filled with infidelity and distrust, and his head is filled with rage and instability.

I've tried to help him over the years, but I can't seem to penetrate his walls. He's locked up tight like Fort Knox, and I know it all started four years ago during that fucked-up summer. Actually, no, it started before that because Brody Landry's house has always been fucked-up, but the summer Kailey left us really changed him.

Between the four of us, I am the closest to Brody. I think he sees similarities in me he can't find in the others. My family is fucked-up and absent, and I've been on antidepressants since freshman year. The difference between us? I take my meds and I want to get better. Brody likes the duality in his mind and really believes he's okay.

He was diagnosed with dissociative identity disorder sophomore year and has been seeing a therapist once a week. At least he was until the beginning of this school year. Then everything changed... Again. Kailey was back in his sights—not that she ever left—and his focus changed. We had plans to run our fathers' companies to the ground, and now he's off feeding his other side.

His other side—the monster in his head, as he calls it—is dangerous and destructive. When Brody was first diagnosed, all four of us went to a few of his therapy sessions so we could be more informed about his condition. We were told there would be bouts of amnesia as he would flip between personalities. His temperament would be volatile, and his mannerisms would be unpredictable.

Most of those things were true. He had extreme mood swings, and he would sometimes change in how he spoke, but I never witnessed a change in his personality until the night his brother was killed. The man I witnessed entering that room holding Georgina wasn't Brody. He looked the same physically, but it was the look in his eyes that was unfamiliar.

I'll never forget that night or the role I played in it afterward. There's nothing I wouldn't do for my brothers, and that sentiment is even stronger for Brody. He's never really had anyone but us three in his corner. He had Kailey too at one point, but like so many others, she left.

When she first turned her back on us, I was angry and full of hatred. I wanted to make her life hell and watch her suffer. The affect her leaving had on each of us was profound. So when Brody set in motion her ostracism, I was one hundred percent on board.

Knowing what I know now though, I wish we had looked into it more. Kailey has been our friend since preschool. We really should've known something happened to her, and it should've been us to protect her. We failed her, and I can only be grateful to Caine and Cooper for killing the pieces of shit that defiled her. I only wish I could bring them back and do it over again, but this time, with my own hands.

I'm on my way home when my phone's vibration hits my thigh. I pull over and reach into my pocket. I see Cooper's name across the screen and put him on speaker.

"Everything okay?" I ask quickly. My heart races at the thought of something happening to Kailey.

"Can you come by Kailey's tonight? We need to talk about some things."

"I can head over now," I say, then hang up.

A few minutes later, I'm pulling into Kailey's driveway. I see Caine outside smoking a joint, and I immediately go to him. He holds out the joint, and I take a hit.

"We need Brody back, man," Caine says as I hand him back the joint.

"I know."

"Look." He takes a hit and passes it back. "They're going to question you inside about where he is. I'm not going to question you because you're just going to tell me. I know you know where he is. I know how tight you two are."

The smoke slowly climbs above my head as I exhale. "I know."

"Well?" he raises a brow.

"He's close. After Justin and Lance, he just needs space. We have to give it to him; you know the consequences of forcing him."

"Fuck." His hand scrubs down his face. "Georgie?"

"You'll have to talk to him about that." I shake my head.

"The girls are asking questions."

"I know, I just left Faith's." I take another hit and pass it back. "I'll see you inside."

I'm grateful for the buzz I have going on. It'll help me dodge the fucking firing line I have waiting for me inside. I close the front door behind me as Oliver steps out of the family room.

"Hey." He nods at me once. "They're waiting for you in there." He thumbs behind him.

"Cool."

I haven't really taken the time to get to know Oliver Ballon, and I can't seem to make myself try. Maybe it's the thought that he's a guidance counselor who's fucking my best friend. *Best friend*, I guess that happened again with no warning.

I brush by him and enter the family room to Cooper smoothing down Kailey's hair as she gnaws on her fingernails. Her eyes look frantic as she quickly stands up and crosses the room toward me.

"Zeke." Her raspy voice jolts my cock awake inside my pants, and I smother a groan into my fist. "I think someone has been in my house."

"Why? What happened?" I ask her, tucking her hair behind her ear before I can stop myself.

"I can feel someone watching me sometimes. I find weird things around the house." She seems unaffected by my touching her, so I curl my hands into fists at my sides.

"What weird things?" I look over at Cooper with my brow raised.

"There was an eaten apple core on the table today," he answers with a shrug.

"And last week!" Kailey exclaims.

"Shit." I wipe my hand down my face and exhale. "That was me... Sorry." I fucking hate apples.

The lie comes easy. That's what happens when you have a lying, no-good piece of shit as a father, you pick up on the habits.

"It was you?" Her hazel eyes are large with worry, and her voice is begging me to confirm the lies.

"Yes." I nod. "I'll try to..."

Before I can finish my sentence, she throws herself into my arms, and my traitorous limbs pull her in tighter against me.

"Thank you," she whispers into my chest.

Fuck, there's no turning back for me. The smell of her hair, the feel of her skin, and the warmth of her body already feels like they're all mine. I don't know exactly what that means, but I have to try my best to fight this shit. I won't be a fourth in this fucking equation.

I grip onto her biceps and ease her back a few paces. More distance, the better.

"Is that all you guys needed?" I ask Cooper because looking at her right now will crumble my whole resolve.

"I think Caine wants to chat with us both."

"Cool. I'll wait for you in the backyard." I nod as I pivot on my heel.

As I walk out of the room, I hear Kailey's soft voice ask Cooper, "Did I do something wrong?"

"No, sha, he's new to our dynamic..." I don't listen to the rest as I stalk outside.

With Caine's constant teasing, and Cooper's faith that we'll all work it out, I feel myself softening. I can't let that happen. I could never be in a relationship where I am sharing the girl I love and watching as another man enjoys her. Yes, in the moment when I'm watching them together, I want to stay... I even want to take part, but what grown ass man wouldn't?

My head is clear when they're not around, and I realize I need to build some distance between us before the fog of lust settles in for good.

"Did you say you ate those apples?"

"What the fuck?" I jump as soon as I hear Brody's voice coming from the left side of her deck.

"Well?" he asks calmly. It only makes me want to hit him more.

"Yeah, can you go fuck off before someone catches you?" I growl into the dark. "If Caine finds this out, he will kill us both."

"Like he did my brother, right?" He sounds angry and maybe a little vengeful.

"Your brother fucking deserved it for what he did to Kailey, and you fucking know it."

All I hear is his snort before the door behind me opens.

"Are you talking to yourself, brother?" Caine's deep tenor cuts through the dark.

"Just talking myself out of a bad idea," I grumble.

"I just wanted to reach out and see if there were any updates," he says as he throws himself into a chair.

I stare across the backyard at the overgrown Wisteria and feel saddened when I see how much of the gazebo is swallowed up by the vines.

"I have a new firm I'm working with this week. If everything pans out, they have a new technology that will shove my father's company into irreparable loss. I will track every single person on his fleet."

The door opens and Cooper joins us on the deck.

"What's new with you this week, Coop?" Caine asks him.

"Oddly enough, I had a company come forward asking for a quote to beat the one my father gave a few months ago."

"What company? And how did they hear about you?" Caine questions him. Fuck, I even want to hear his answer to this, knowing it was all Brody.

"They are an affiliate of the Ballon's and need a new clean-up crew. Their previous one botched a murder scene and a few of their big guns got life." He exhales loudly. "I need to talk to Oliver and find out if it was him that suggested my company."

"How would Ballon know about you?" Caine asks.

"He has resources we don't even know about. Do you think it's time we brought him into the fold?" Cooper inquires.

I knew it would be just a matter of time. They are brother-husbands, after all. I know I sound bitter as fuck, and I need to see this through unbiased eyes. Yes, Ballon would be an asset to us with everything he was trained for and what he can get his hands on.

"We'll take a vote when Brody reappears," Caine affirms.

"What's been goin' on at the assassin HQ?" Cooper asks Caine.

"I have a new recruit, and weirdly, he's a distant cousin."

"What? How the hell did that work out?" Cooper chuckles.

"His family sent him here. Something about him acting up in Canada. He's staying with my mother's sister and her family. After that, I don't have a clue how he found me. He's a monster though. Tall and fucking built like a tank."

"What's his name? How old is he?" I ask.

"Daniel, he likes to go by Danny, and he's our age. He's finishing up high school online and refuses to attend school. Which works perfectly."

"Not bad." I shrug and look around. Brody is either nearby listening like the fucking stalker he is, or he left as soon as the guys came out.

"When are you going to give in?" Caine looks at me with a smirk.

"To what?" I raise my brow.

"To your feelings. We can see it. You want her too," Cooper says, and I hear a fucking snort come from behind me.

"Snort all you want." Caine chuckles. "You can try to fight it a while longer. Just know we'll be here saying we told you so later."

Fucking Brody is still in this yard, and I know I'll be hearing an earful of this later.

"Just friends, man." I shrug and start for the door. "Can I go now?"

"Yeah," Caine says. "If you hear from him, let us know."

"Sure," I call over my shoulder and go back inside the house.

As I walk by the family room, I hear murmuring inside. I guess Oliver is in there with her, and since the others are here, I can get my ass home. Where I should be, far enough away from her and the way she smells.

"Going home?" Her voice hits my back, and I can feel the ripples make their way up the back of my neck.

"Yeah," I say over my shoulder, not bothering to turn around.

"You'll be here tomorrow?"

I tip my head to the ceiling and slowly turn around. "Bebelle, maybe it's best if I catch up on some work. I'll be by to check on you in a few days."

Her hazel eyes close as her chin drops to her chest. "You're running."

"What do you mean?" I know exactly what she means, and she's right.

"You're pulling away. Was it something I did?" Her voice is small, and she's still looking at the floor.

I can't stand to see her like this, not after everything she's been through. I can't be the one to add any more pain to what she already has.

"Bebelle," I say softly, gripping her chin in my hand, and forcing her to look at me. "It's nothing you did; I just need to work some things out up here." I point to my head.

Her hazel eyes shine with unshed tears, and I watch as she sucks that full lower lip into her mouth. My fingers release her chin, but only to glide along the soft skin of her jaw and then sink into the thick waves of her hair. When I have a firm grip on the back of her head, I haul her in and press my forehead to hers.

"Zeke?"

I don't know if it's the sound of her voice or the warmth of her breath, but I lift my head and press my mouth to hers. It's soft, and I drag her bottom lip into my mouth, then move to the top.

Her moan, and then the feel of hands moving along my sides, changes everything. I will allow myself this one taste and then never again. So I decide to make it worth it. Both of my hands slide into her hair, and I grip her head between them. I angle her head, and then I'm plunging into her mouth.

My teeth clink against hers and my tongue roughly glides in, tangling with hers. It's everything I've dreamed of and more.

Her taste, her sounds, and her plush mouth are fucking euphoric. Her hands fist in my shirt, and I feel her pulling me in closer, her body pressing into mine.

That's it, that's as far as I can take it before I hit the no return mark. I rip my mouth from hers and wince at her whimper. Then, like the asshole I am, I turn my back on her and leave the fucking house.

KAILEY HIMARI

FIVE

I stand watching Zeke leave with my fingertips pressed against my swollen lips. I tentatively lick my tongue along them to taste the last remnants of him. I close my eyes and savor it, knowing it will probably never happen again.

"He'll come around." I jump at the sound of Oliver's voice and slowly turn to face him.

"I'm sure that was just a one-time thing," I whisper as I search his face. What is he thinking? Did I just cheat on him? On all of them?

"You look worried," he says with a slight smile.

"I'm s-sorry that happened. It's s-supposed to be just us four." I'm stuttering as I try to explain my actions. "I've always c-cared about him, and I'm s-scared I'm losing him again."

Oliver stalks forward, his face as stern as always and his golden skin making his silver eyes pop.

"Kail, I once said to you I don't mind sharing as long as I get to have you too. The sentiment still stands. Only now, I love you, and if he makes you happy too, then fuck it, he's welcome."

"I doubt it will ever come to that," I squeal as he grabs me around the waist and picks me up. My legs lock behind him and my arms curl around his neck.

"Whatever makes you happy, baby," he mutters as he kisses my neck. "Want to know what'll make me happy?"

"What will make you happy, Mr. Ballon?"

His only reply is a growl that works its way from his chest and out through his mouth. Then that gorgeous mouth is on mine. His hands grab my ass in handfuls as he guides me upstairs and to my room.

When we get inside, I see the still rumpled bed from me and Cooper, but Oliver doesn't care as he lies both of us down and thoroughly explores my mouth with his tongue. His hands slip under my shirt as he slowly drags it up, his palms running along my skin. Goose bumps break out along my arms as his mouth moves from mine and settles in that sweet spot just behind my ear.

His head dips down as he bites my nipple through the thin lace of my bra, my body trembling with anticipation. Oliver knows how to add just the right amount of pain to make it pleasurable. My shirt is removed, and I moan as his hands pull down my leggings.

He pushes up on to his hands and stares down at me. "I love you."

"Yeah?" I grin at him. "Show me just how much."

I press myself against him, then frown when I feel his slacks and dress shirt. He gets up onto his knees between my legs, then slowly undoes his pants button and zipper. His cock is pressing against the opening and fighting with the fabric of his boxers. My pussy floods at the sight and I need to feel him inside me.

He pulls his pants off, then chuckles when he sees the frustration painted clearly on my face. "Do you know one of the most important things I tell my students?"

"Oliver…" I groan, my patience wearing thin.

"That's Mr. Ballon to you." He runs his finger up my center, pressing against my panties. "Do I need to repeat my question, Miss Richard?"

Oh, fuck. Guidance counselor Oliver gets me so ramped up and hot, I can barely think.

He leans back down onto his hands and brings his mouth to my ear. "Punishment is not a detention in this room, Miss Richard. Do. I. Need. To. Repeat. My. Question?"

Each word is punctuated by the grind of his hips against mine, and I tip my head back and moan, "No, Mr. Ballon. I don't know what you tell your students." My voice is soft and filled with lust.

"Patience is a virtue." He moves back up to kneeling, and the grin on his face is absolutely sinful.

"Fuck patience," I say, sitting up in front of him. My hands reach out to rip his dress shirt off, the buttons flying in all directions.

"Wrong answer." He *tsks*, then his body is on top of mine, pressing into all the right places.

"Punish me," I beg, biting hard into my lip.

Oliver has a side to him I can feel he holds back. I know it's because of what he's seen happen to me and what he knows happened to me. But I want him to be completely himself, and I want him to be free.

"Kail…"

"Do it, Mr. Ballon."

At my words, his face grows serious, his finger gliding down my torso. "You're sure?"

"Do. I. Have. To. Repeat. Myself?" I throw back at him as his face lights up with a devious smile.

He rips my bra down the center, revealing my breasts, and flips me over onto my stomach. "What's your safeword with Caine?" Everyone knows Caine is the dominating asshole of our equation.

"I don't have one."

His quick intake of breath betrays his surprise, and he props my hips up, pulling me up to my knees. He can't be any worse than Caine… Right?

His fingers slip into the back of my thong, and he rips them off my body in one rough pull. Then I feel him pushing his way inside me, and I thank God I was ready to go.

This position always brings a slightly panicky feeling at first, but I've learned to concentrate on the smell and feeling of who's behind me. I move with him, moaning loudly as he pulls out and slowly thrusts back in. Not nearly as bad as Caine. This is nothing…

It's then that I feel the fabric of my thong being slipped over my head and wrapped around my neck.

"Did you think that was it?" His breath hits my neck and ear. "I'm just getting started, Kail. Did you want to rethink that safeword?"

I shake my head and gasp when I feel him tighten his

hold on the lace around my neck. My air supply lessens but his strokes intensify, creating a panic-induced arousal. My pussy is so wet, the fluids sliding down my thighs, and the noises it's making is almost embarrassing.

He slams into me, punishing me for defying him, and then he pulls back on the thong around my neck, making my head bend backwards. It's uncomfortable, but I can't bring myself to tell him to stop. I don't even think I'm able to.

I can't breathe. This is where I should panic, but instead, I'm clenching around his hard cock. Blackness bleeds in around the edges of my vision, making me helpless to do anything but feel the explosion wrack my body as I try to gulp air.

"Almost a minute now, Kail." His voice is taunting, nothing like the Oliver I know. "Think you can do two?"

I want to shake my head, but the intensity of my orgasm wins out over my need to stay alive.

He hasn't slowed down his thrusting. No, if anything, he's increased his speed, as he continues to make me struggle for air. My lungs ache, and my hand reaches up to the cloth around my neck. I can feel the deep imprint it's leaving in my skin.

I want to tell him to stop… I want to tell him to go harder. My thoughts are a mixed jumble of needing air and wanting to come again.

I am nearly to the point of passing out. My vision is gray and my chest is constricting when I feel myself coming again. It's so intense, and I'm helpless as I ride the wave, accepting that I may very well die here tonight.

"Fuck, yes." I can hear Oliver, but he sounds like he's underwater.

Just as my vision goes completely black, I feel the lace loosen and I'm instinctively sucking in gulps of air. My throat burns from the rough fabric, my chest burns from lack of oxygen, and my pussy is throbbing from the most intense orgasm I have had yet.

"I'm… going… to… kill… you…" I get out between coughing and gasping.

"Safewords are important," he says from behind me as he rubs my back. "I knew when to let go."

I shake my head and lie there uselessly as his cum slides out of me. My body is still tingling, coming down from the high of not being able to breathe and an orgasm that has rocked me to my fucking core.

I reach up and touch the tender spot around my throat where the fabric bit into the skin. It's slightly swollen, and I groan as I imagine yet another mark on my body. Caine's teeth and fingerprints just weren't enough… I had to add Oliver's kink for strangulation.

Regardless, I can't seem to convince myself to hate it, and as sadistic as it sounds, I want to see what else he likes to do.

"Are you okay?" He lies beside me and rubs a soothing pattern into my ass cheek.

"If I say yes, how soon can we do it again?"

He barks out a laugh and leans in to take my earlobe between his teeth. "Let's just take our time."

"You're like Jekyll and Hyde." I smile at him.

"Mr. Ballon and Oliver?" His eyes dance with mirth, and I giggle into his arm.

"Let's shower and clean ourselves up, then change the sheets because you made a mess." I watch as he gets up from the bed in all his naked glory and pads toward the bathroom.

I lift my body and groan when I feel the sheet stuck to my chest and stomach. I guess I did make a mess.

After my shower and covering my throat with a good turtleneck, I head downstairs to find Caine and Cooper speaking low in the kitchen. As soon as I enter, they both stop and watch me closely.

"Is this about Brody?" I ask as I grab a bottle of water out of the fridge.

Caine just gives me a smirk, and Cooper eyes my outfit. "Chilly?" He snickers.

"Did Oliver teach his student a lesson?" Caine adds, and they both erupt into laughter.

I can't hold in the grin that comes over my face and a part of me is happy they are so at ease with our situation.

"I kissed Zeke," I blurt out of nowhere, and they both suddenly stop laughing.

"Did he like it?" Cooper's face is one of shock.

I sit down in a chair with a huff and roll my eyes. "I think so? Anyway, it was a one-time thing. I'm sorry, I wasn't expecting for it to happen."

"Twenty bucks." Caine holds his hand out to Cooper.

"Fuck," Cooper groans and slaps a twenty in his hand.

"What's going on?" I look between them both.

"I just lost a bet." Cooper shrugs and leans back in his chair.

"What bet?" My voice is getting shriller as this conversation progresses.

"Breathe, sha." Cooper places his hand on my forearm. "We were just betting on how long it would take for Zeke to..."

"Cross over to the dark side," Caine finishes for him and flashes me a devious grin.

"You guys are seriously dumb. He's not." I get up from the table and watch as a freshly showered Oliver strides in.

"Who's not?" he asks as he leans against the counter.

"Sha doubts her allure," Cooper explains as he stands and stretches. His shirt pulls up, and I get a delicious look at the Adonis belt leading to the waistband of his jeans.

"Ah, Zeke?" Oliver says with a chuckle.

"He's stubborn," Caine adds. "But he'll come around."

"Hold on," I cut in. "Are y'all holding open auditions for spots in our relationship?"

"No," Caine growls, and it's the first look of jealousy I've seen yet. "Zeke is our brother, and trust me, ma petite. We see how you both look at each other."

"Or how you kiss each other," Oliver interjects with a smirk.

"I'm going to bed." I shake my head.

I can't think about these things right now. I already have enough shit going on. Besides, my body is worn out from the abundance of sex, and my head is swimming with worries.

"Tomorrow is the last day of school before the holiday break. Why don't you go up and get some rest for tomorrow? Everything will work itself out." Oliver wraps his arm around my shoulders and kisses my temple.

"Ma petite," Caine calls out as I turn to leave the kitchen. "We already feel like Zeke is one of us."

I don't know why him saying that calms my swirling stomach. Zeke doesn't want any part of this.

BRODY

SIX

I hate my fucking house. I hate everyone that's ever lived in it, and that includes myself. Every room and every corridor remind me of a childhood memory, and none of them are good. The front foyer: where I watched my father beat my mother for the first time. The family room: where I watched him fuck a woman that wasn't my mother. Then my room: where my mother laid a pillow over my face but changed her mind… Just to name a few.

Walking through this house also reminds me of Kailey. She's made memories here too, but I doubt she even thinks of them anymore. I can remember a few. She ran out of my pool house into the night when she caught Georgie and me fooling around. I can remember coming up here to the main house later, and hearing my brother laughing along as a guy described her giving blowjobs in the forest.

I dragged Georgie back into that pool house, and we lost our virginity that night. Maybe I was saving it for Kails, but she ruined it by being a slut. Was she a slut then? I'm not sure. I grab my hair in both of my hands and pull. She says Lance and Justin defiled her, ruined her against her will. Did they? I don't know.

Is she a slut now? Yes. She opens her legs and gives herself away to multiple guys each day. Am I fixated because I wanted to have that? Or am I still feeling discarded as she forgives the others? I'm disappointed, but that's what everyone around me does. They disappoint and shatter any illusions I have about their decency. So do I believe Justin and Lance raped Kail? I believe they were capable of it, as was anyone else.

This house is a mess. I haven't permitted the cleaning staff in here for the last three months, and my parents won't be around until I graduate. They'll want to show face, then my mother will fly back to her boyfriend in the Caribbean somewhere, and my father back to whichever mistress he chooses. When Justin was killed, they came home and buried him. They told everyone there was a terrible car accident and then disappeared again, leaving me here to parent myself.

No one but me has been here for three months, and it works because every time my best friends come looking for me, the house appears deserted. Justin was the only one who shared my blood that cared. My only genuine family, and he was killed because of the accusations made by a girl who loves to spread her legs.

My room is dark and cold, like me. I throw my sweater to the side, and watch as it misses the chair, hitting the floor in another messy heap. My room is a maze of messy heaps, and I can't bring myself to care.

It takes a lot of energy to care, and since I misplaced my prescription, I don't have the energy. Besides, I don't even need it. I was only taking it to calm those around me, and to maintain my position. If people knew what my diagnosis was, they would run in the other direction. I have a firm grip on the monster and he's not getting out unless I let him.

I lie on my bed and grab my phone, opening the app I'm looking for, and suddenly Kails' room is playing on my screen. It takes me a minute, but finally I understand what I'm watching. Kails is being choked and fucked by none other than Mr. Ballon. I thought this was more of Caine's thing, but I was wrong.

I watch as he tightens his hold on the strap around her neck, and rethink everything I thought I knew about him. I thought he was the odd one out, the one who stayed on the sidelines and didn't disrupt the dynamic. I can admit when I'm wrong, but this shit… This is aggressive, and Kails looks nothing like a victim of rape. I watch as she comes on his dick, all the while trying to fucking breathe.

I throw my phone to the side, then slip my hand into my pants. The monster is growling and scratching at my skin, but I shove him back. I can't let Kails being fucked by one of her many men bother me. I let that girl go a long fucking time ago.

I stroke my cock and tip my head back at the sensation. I can't help it. I envision Kails riding me and moaning as I stretch her wide. She was my first fantasy the very first time I popped a boner. Seventh year, my birthday pool party. She walked out of my house in a white bikini, and my dick decided she was what it wanted. I was just a kid with an attractive girl in front of me.

Now, as I leisurely stroke my cock, I envision her sinking down on top of me, her pussy so wet and the juices running down over my balls. She arches her back, and her hair brushes my thighs as she moves. Small rotations of her hips, my hands grabbing her tits, and her moans sounding throughout my room.

She picks up the pace. My balls are saturated in her wetness as her pussy clenches around my cock, pulling the orgasm forward. I try to hold back, keep the momentum going, but it's been a while, and I can't stop the jerk of cum squirting from my cock. The ropes of white land on my stomach, and I groan at the warm feeling.

I think it's time for Kails and I to have a face-to-face.

KAILEY HIMARI

SEVEN

School is the same shit it's always been, but in the past few months, people don't bother me, and the hounds stay firmly away. Without their bitch leader, they tend to just run in circles and try to catch their own tails.

Being connected to the Golden Four has its own set of problems. Now, everyone is trying to be polite to me, but I can see how shallow it is, because as soon as the guys are out of sight, I'm back to being nothing. I will admit, being nothing is a lot better than being hated, and I thoroughly enjoy a clean locker.

The parking lot is bustling this morning as Cooper parks his Wrangler. I look around and see Caine's truck parked beside Zeke's motorcycle. I smile when I see them both watching the Wrangler. I'm glad Zeke is here, and he's not avoiding me.

Oliver is also here somewhere. He's faculty, so he comes in an hour before the bell, and he stays away save for our bi-weekly meetings. Speaking of, I have one of those meetings today and I can't help the excitement I feel when I think about it. Sitting in a small office, the door unlocked and the risk of being caught heightening the arousal. I'm waiting for when we give into the temptation and rip each other's clothes off on school property.

"Zeke seems all right," I murmur to Cooper.

"Don't think too hard about it, sha." He grabs my hand and places a sweet kiss on my palm.

We get out of the Wrangler, then Cooper takes my hand again as we walk over to Zeke and Caine.

"Ma petite," Caine growls, then pulls me into his arms. His hand fists into my hair and his nose hits my throat as he inhales deeply. "I want to fuck you so bad right now."

Typical Caine with his crass words making my panties wet all hours of the day.

"Wow," Zeke mutters, then walks off ahead of us into the school.

Caine chuckles as he throws his arm over my shoulders and steers me toward the entrance. As we walk in, the first thing I see is Casey and Connie standing off to the side as Faith's mouth is being swallowed up by Zeke. My stomach flips, and I feel a burning sensation working its way up my chest. Jealousy is a potent feeling, and right now it's all-consuming.

I want to rip them apart, then rip the very hair out of their scalps. I'm so angry, and I clench my teeth to keep myself from reacting. If only she knew that tongue was just down my throat in the last twelve hours.

"Looks like he'll be coming around sooner rather than later." Cooper chuckles as he fist bumps Caine.

I ignore them because talking right now is next to

impossible, but if I could speak, I would tell them just how idiotic they are. Zeke is clearly replacing our moment with one he'd rather have, and as hard as it is to admit, he and Faith make a perfect pair.

I shrug out of Caine's hold and make my way to my locker. I hear Casey and Connie snicker behind me, but that's all they've had the balls to do lately.

"Boo!" Her voice automatically calms me, and I turn toward the sound. Kimmy's arms circle around my shoulders, and I sink into her comforting warmth. This is exactly what I needed.

"Thank you," I say into her big hair. "I love you."

She pulls back and lifts my wrist to watch my Gris-Gris swing back and forth. "I'm happy you're still wearing this."

Kimmy still has no idea about anything that went down with Justin or Lance, and I want to keep it that way. Yes, she's my very best friend, but I feel like telling her now would make me have to rehash everything from the beginning.

"It's working." I smile at her.

"So, New Year's!" She squeals a little and prances on the spot. "There's a masked ball, and I want us all to go!"

"Sounds fun." I grin at her excitement.

"I'm sending you the link tonight. We have to buy our tickets before they sell out."

"Uh… Does Henry know about my um… Situation?" I ask her as I bite my lip.

"What?" She giggles. "Your many boyfriends? One of which is a guidance counselor?"

"Shhhh!"

"Yeah, he knows, and he says not to give me any ideas because he can't share," she pouts, and the look is adorable.

"You two are perfect the way you are." I shake my head and laugh at her.

"We are." She shrugs, and I laugh again.

"Sha!" Cooper calls out. "We'll see you at lunch."

I nod at him and blush when Caine throws me a heated look. Insatiable, that one.

"Sheesh," Kimmy breathes. "Does he always look like he wants to devour you?"

"Yeah, he does," Zeke answers from behind me, and I startle at his voice.

"I got to get to my dang locker. See you at lunch," Kimmy says, and leaves me alone with Zeke.

I'm instantly feeling awkward, and the air around us is saturated with it.

"Look—" he starts, but I cut him off.

"Everything is fine, Zeke. Let's not make this weird." I open my locker and grab out my books.

"Cool," he mumbles and visibly relaxes. "I'll see you at lunch."

I nod, watching as he turns and walks in the opposite direction. His gelled faux hawk gleaming under the fluorescent lights and his tattoo covered arms swinging at his sides. I can't help but watch him walk away.

"That one you can't have." Faith.

"I don't want him," I shrug and slam my locker closed.

"Yeah, sure," she sneers. "That's why you're salivating

over him."

"Faith, you guys look stronger than ever. Stop acting desperate… It stinks." I scrunch up my nose and walk away.

I *was* fucking salivating for him, if the pools of it in my mouth are any indication.

Lunch has me sitting between Caine and Cooper, with Kimmy across from us, and Zeke sucking more face with Faith. I can't stop the acid pool of jealousy from flooding my insides and stealing my appetite. I shove my tray away forcefully, then lay my head on my arms with a huff.

"Ma petite, eat more than that," Caine urges, as he nudges my arm.

"Not hungry," I groan into my sweater.

The bell rings, signaling the end of lunch, and I sigh with relief… I can't continue to watch this shit all day. I have one thing to look forward to, the announcement that will pull me out of class and into my guidance counselor's office. My *boyfriend's* office. Maybe I will work off this frustration I'm suddenly feeling.

"You have work tonight?" Cooper asks, and I groan.

"Yes."

"I'll drop you off and one of us will pick you up. Closing again?"

"Yes, ten thirty, I should be done."

"Okay." He kisses the side of my head. "We'll figure it out."

I get up from the table and stalk off ahead of anyone else. I'm in no mood to speak about anything.

"If it bothers you, why not add another to the mix?" Kimmy's amused voice hits the back of my head.

"Not bothered."

"Not hungry, not bothered. Why are you speaking like a cave dweller then?" She snickers.

I stop and turn to look her in the eye. "It's just not that easy. I'm not out to keep increasing my numbers, and this thing between Zeke and me is just confusing right now."

She sees the distress on my face and pulls me in for a hug. "Well, hell, I'm sorry for making light of the situation."

"It's fine." I pull away, and we walk side by side down the hallway. "I'll see you after school?"

"Kay, boo." She nods, then hurries off in the opposite direction.

I walk into my next class with lead feet and an aching heart. This situation with Zeke is really messing with my emotions, and I can't seem to figure out what I want. You would think three boyfriends are more than enough and looking at how to fit a fourth is just ridiculous. But what if that fourth owns just as much a part of your soul as the others?

Much of my class is spent stressing over my feelings, then about how the guys are feeling, and it takes my teacher three tries to get my attention.

"Guidance." She smiles, and I get up out of my seat with a nod.

When Oliver and I aren't flirting our way through our one-hour sessions, he makes me talk about what happened in those woods, the situation with my father, and our unconventional relationship. As much as I enjoy the tension and the excitement of being together at school, I really need to pick his brain about Zeke.

I knock on his door and enter when he calls me inside.

"Hey, gorgeous." His smile is wide, and his steel-gray eyes shine with happiness.

"Hello, Mr. Ballon." I watch as those eyes darken with desire, and my insides vibrate with want.

"I can hear the sadness in your voice. Did you want to talk to me about it?" Always so perceptive.

"It's about Zeke."

"Ah, Ezekiel Boudreaux." His smile stays firmly in place, and I breathe a sigh of relief.

"I hate seeing him with Faith," I groan as I plop down into a seat.

"That's his girlfriend." He raises a brow at me.

"I know that! But he just had his tongue in my mouth last night!"

"It's probably just as confusing for him seeing us with you," he counters, leaning back in his chair.

"I doubt it. He was all over her today."

"Question." A mischievous smile ghosts his lips. "What if he wanted to see you both?"

I can see what he's doing here, and I can admit when I'm being selfish as fuck. I know my guys share me without issue, even encourage it, but I can't share them with another girl. Just the thought of it drives me wild with jealousy.

"No," I growl.

Oliver chuckles and gets up out of his chair to come over to me. He kneels in front of my chair and brushes his knuckles over my cheek.

"You need to talk to him, Kail."

"I'm scared he doesn't feel the same, and I'll ruin our friendship again." I sniff.

"Would you rather live with these feelings? Imagine when he gets married or has children. What then?" Imagining that makes me feel ill, and my empty stomach cramps. I drop my face into my hands and groan.

"I don't know how to say it."

"It'll come naturally. Just let your feelings guide you," he suggests soothingly.

"Thank you, Oliver." I lift my head and lean over to kiss him softly.

ZEKE

EIGHT

I'm waiting for her outside of the restaurant. Cooper roped me into picking her up, telling me, he and Caine have a video game marathon going on, and Oliver is sorting some shit out with his family.

I didn't want to come here, but I didn't want to leave her stranded either. It's hard to think when she's close, and I end up making mistakes. Like watching her plump lips frown when she thinks no one is watching, or when her eyebrows come together when she's deep in thought. I know—as much as she's trying to pretend—she's still not recovered from what happened to her. Not that I expect her to be. I just hope she's not hiding it from us.

I get off my bike and go to lean against the brick of the restaurant wall. If it was up to me, I wouldn't let Kailey work at all, especially knowing what I do and who's been watching her. I want to believe that Brody is harmless, but I saw what he did to someone he called a traitor, and I know the betrayal he's feeling toward Kailey is much worse.

I hear the bell of the door opening and watch as Kailey steps out into the dark. Her hair is up in a tight bun, and she smells like cooking oil.

"These waitress uniforms are getting duller every year." I chuckle.

Her reaction is quick. She drops her purse and throws her hands in the air as her voice breaks through the night with a shrill scream. The fear in her eyes has my breath catching and I immediately feel like a damn idiot.

"Fuck, Kailey, I'm sorry." I try to reach for her, but she stumbles back a few steps. She's shaking her head profusely and her mouth is gaping as she tries to find her words. "Shit, I didn't think." I'm trying and fucking failing at my attempt to calm her.

She hasn't blinked, her chest is rising and falling rapidly, and I'm afraid she's going to pass out at any moment. Her skin is a scary gray shade, and I'm worried I've given her a heart attack.

"Ze-Zeke?" She finally speaks, her voice hoarse from her scream.

"I'm sorry." I cover my face with my hand. "I'm so fucking stupid."

Her hands move to her chest, and she drops her head as she tries to regulate her breathing. She's been on edge these last few months, and rightfully so after all she's been through, but I tend to forget it because she acts like nothing has happened to her.

When she looks up, I see her eyes fading like she's watching a movie and not standing right here in front of me. I rush over to her, despite her panic, and grab her face between both of my hands.

"Kailey," I whisper, and drop my face to hers. My lips brush against her cheek, and I hear her whimper. "Don't go back there. Stay here with me."

Her body is rigid, and I can feel her slowly slipping away into the dark crevices of her mind. I do the only thing I can think of that will keep her here in the present. I brush my nose along her cheek and press my lips softly to hers.

She gasps, and I take that opportunity to run my tongue along her open lips, tasting her. I kiss her bottom lip, taking extra care to brush it with my tongue, then move to her top lip, doing the same. Finally, her body relaxes, and I feel her hands press against my chest. I pull away because I'm not sure if she's pushing me away, but just as confusing as she is, her hands grab my shirt and she's pulling me in again.

This time, the kiss is rougher, messier, and fucking sinful. Our mouths are angled and opened wide as we come together, leaving no space between us. Her curves press against me, and I moan so deeply it's startling.

This is what passion feels like, like a building heat that's on the brink of exploding, and you're just waiting, hoping you survive the aftermath. This is what I've always been searching for.

Her hands end up cupping my face, and mine are gripping her ass. I rub my painfully hard cock into her stomach, and she moans heartily. We've always had the potential for this, for an all-consuming fire, but it was cut short. I don't want it to be cut short again. I want her, and I'm realizing it doesn't matter if the others have her too. Kailey-Himari Richard is meant to be mine.

I break apart from her lips and chuckle as she leans forward, chasing after mine. "Let me take you home." My voice is husky and deep.

She immediately looks dejected, and my heart sinks. Of

course, this is awkward. I can't just waltz in the house and expect the guys to be all for it. "You're going to run." She sounds sad and resigned as she picks her purse up.

"What?"

"This is when you realize this was another mistake and disappear again. I played the same game with Oliver. I know the signs." She turns and walks toward my bike.

"Bebelle." I chase after her. "What do you want?"

She stops, keeping her back to me, and I watch as her shoulders rise on an inhale. "I want you. I've always wanted you, Zeke." Her words are soft, and if I wasn't standing right behind her, I wouldn't have heard them.

"Do I have to fill out a form? Be interviewed by the others?" I'm joking but also not, I don't know what their agreement is.

"Just take me home." She still sounds sad, and I don't know what to say to change that. Maybe adding me to the mix is something she doesn't want to do. I grab my helmet and push it down over her head. It stops at the bun and goes no farther. "Wait." She pulls her hair out, and I watch as the unruly waves tumble down her back in a sea of chestnut brown. "What about you?"

"I'll be fine. It's not far." I shrug.

I throw my leg over the bike and sit, waiting for her to get on behind me. I'm not prepared for it when she does. Her heat seeps through my clothes, and her scent engulfs me. I take a deep breath and try not to groan like a horny teenager when her hands encircle my waist.

I start the bike and try my best to concentrate on the road, but how the fuck does someone do that without trying not to imagine the heat of her pussy on their lower back? Her hands fist into my shirt, and I grin, knowing the effects of the vibrations. But what fucking shocks me and almost puts us in a ditch is her hand slowly reaching under my shirt and stroking the skin of my abs.

Yeah, I'm done.

I pull the bike over, cut the engine, and release the kickstand.

"Zeke?"

"Get off." I know I sound harsh, but I can't fucking help it.

I feel the absence of her warmth instantly, but I know it'll all be worth it in the end. I get off the bike and stand in front of her, my chest rising and falling with each breath, then I rip the helmet off her head, throwing it aside.

Her eyes are wide with apprehension, but when they meet mine, something in them flares. I don't give her any warning as my hands grab her hair, and our mouths are fused back together.

It's in that moment, the sky opens up and a sheet of rain drenches us in an instant. It doesn't deter us. The onslaught just drives us closer together, and at this point, I'm feeling like it's still not close enough. I want her skin on mine, and I can't wait to get her anywhere else. Here will have to do.

"I don't plan on stopping. This is your only chance to back out," I warn as I pull my lips off hers, my hands firmly gripping her ass.

She looks up at me through her rain-soaked lashes. "Don't stop, Zeke."

She asked for it.

I grab her face again and dive into her mouth. She tastes like home, like I've finally found my way out of the overgrown maze. I back her up until her ass hits my bike, and she gasps, her hands landing on the seat to keep her balance.

I pull back and look at her from head to toe, realizing something I've fantasized about but never got around to trying. I grab her arm and turn her around slowly. Her back touches my chest. I kiss her neck and run my tongue along the beads of water running down. She moans and reaches back to grab my thighs, arching her ass into my cock.

I'm hard, probably the hardest I've ever been, and I can't help but grind harder against her. I want to be inside her, and I want it now. I run my hands down her sides and around her front, settling on her zipper. She groans and shoves my hands aside, then she's pulling her pants down in record time.

She turns back around to face me, but I stop her with a hand on her shoulder and guide her back to face my bike. Then, with my hand in the center of her shoulder blades, I push her forward and groan when her hands land on the seat.

Seeing her like this, bent over with her fingertips pressing into the seat, is hot as fuck. Her pink pussy peeks out at me from between her legs, but that's not enough… I want to see more. I step into her and tap her feet apart with my own. I bend over her back and brush her hair out of the way. As soon as I touch her, she tenses up, and I need to decide right now.

Do I continue this, knowing what she's been through? Or do I stop, and let her do what makes her comfortable? Most guys would stop, but I'm not most guys, and I know this woman. She needs to be pushed past her limits sometimes.

I open my belt buckle, letting it hit my thighs, and the noise startles her. I pop my button and lower the zipper slowly. I want her on the edge of sanity. I let my pants and boxers drop in one, then look down at the angry head of my cock. The gleam of metal twinkles up at me through the raindrops—the top of my Jacob's Ladder—I'm a fucking sucker for pain.

I reach over her, letting my cock brush her ass, and reach into the back compartment on my bike for my stash of condoms. Faith can be spontaneous, and we like to fuck in forests or restaurant bathrooms. I don't want to be thinking about my girlfriend of nearly four years right now. Yeah, it's been off and on, but right now, we're kind of on.

I pull out a condom and lower it slowly over the six separate bars along my shaft. That's not including the ring through the tip. I kick her legs farther apart and sink two fingers into her heat. Fuck, she's so fucking wet. I pump into her a few times and grin as she whimpers. She has no idea what she's gotten herself into.

I grip her ass in both hands, spreading her wide, and then I'm pushing into her slowly, making sure she feels every bump. The rain slows down to a drizzle, and I look up to the clearing sky. Typical Louisiana weather.

"Zeke," she pants, and her head falls forward. "What kind of condom is this?"

"Why?" I chuckle softly, pulling her ass back, then sinking in until my balls feel her wetness.

"It feels different. Bumpy," she moans when I withdraw and push back in harder.

"Those are my piercings."

"Oh, fuck," she breathes, and I pick up the pace. I want her cream all over my cock.

Her noises are getting louder, and my balls are growing tighter. I thought if I ever had the chance with Kailey that I would take my time, savor everything, but right now, I find myself chasing her orgasm and my own with unstoppable speed.

I look down and watch as I pull out my cock, the condom saturated with her juices. I groan and pump a few shallow thrusts into her, making sure those piercings are hitting her in all the right spots.

She clamps down hard and screams my name into the trees in front of us. My relief is surprising, glad she isn't screaming one of her boyfriend's names instead. I slow my thrusts and watch as her pussy contracts around my cock, her juices dripping down to the ground below.

"Stop," she breathes as I thrust into her again. She stands up straight, and I step back. Why am I fucking stopping?

"Bebelle…" It's a warning. I clench my jaw to stop myself from saying something rude.

"Sorry, I just want to see these piercings up close." She drops to her knees and reaches for my cock.

I watch as she removes the condom and chucks it to the side. Then she's lifting my cock and staring at the piercings that decorate it. I can't stop the groan that escapes when she strokes it, and I pump my hips into her hand.

"This must've been painful." She's still looking at it in awe as I pump myself into her hand again. I didn't stop just so she could look at it. She's either sucking me off, or I'm bending her back over my bike.

She looks up at my face, and I guess she can read my thoughts because her mouth fuses around the tip. I feel her tongue swipe around the ring through the top, and it takes everything not to come right here and now.

She relaxes her jaw, and I bite my lip as my cock disappears down her throat, one inch at a fucking time. I grab her soaked hair in handfuls and pull her head in faster. I want to come, and I want to come now.

She hasn't taken her eyes off mine, and I smile when I see tears slip out of them, running down her cheeks. I'm rough, I know this, and I know those piercings don't feel so good hitting the back of her throat. It doesn't matter because I can't stop, and I don't think I would even if I could.

She gags for the third time, and I know this isn't her first rodeo. I would guess Caine makes this mouth his favorite pastime. I remove my hands from the sides of her head and place one on the top, firmly gripping her hair. My fingers run through her tears, gathering them, then sucking the fingers into my mouth. It should be every man's favorite treat to taste the tears of the girl he's fucking.

With her salty taste on my tongue, I slam back into her mouth and come. My cum squirts as it hits the back of her throat, and my crying girl swallows every fucking drop. I want to scream her name like she did mine, but I hold it in. I'm just not there yet.

I pull my softening cock out of her mouth and turn to gather our clothing. I grab the used condom off the ground because it's unsanitary and I don't fucking litter. She hasn't said anything, and I watch her closely as she dresses.

I hear the distinct breaking of twigs and the crunch of leaves, telling me we aren't alone.

"Did you hear that?" Her eyes widen and she looks around, quickly doing up her fly.

"Probably an animal." I shrug, but I know differently.

"Can we get out of here?" Her teeth are chattering and she's clutching a ridiculous Gris-Gris in her palm.

"Did that fall off?" I point to the red pouch.

"Yes." She glances around. "I need to get home and find a new strap."

"Okay." I pick up the helmet and put it back on her head, then we get on the bike.

The drive to the house is quick. We were only about five minutes away when we stopped. The house looks dark, but I see Cooper's bright yellow Wrangler parked in the drive. They're probably still playing their marathon and didn't bother to turn the lights on as day slipped into night.

Bebelle gets off the bike, and I grin when I see her stumble, then walk with a slight wobble. I fucking did that. She pulls the helmet off her head and frowns at me.

"Aren't you coming in?" she asks, her voice filled with doubt.

"No." I shake my head and take my helmet out of her hand. "After what just happened, I need to break up with my girlfriend."

"Oh." Her eyes round and she nods. "Right."

"I'll come by in the morning. If you need me, call me," I tell her with a grin.

"Okay," she whispers and turns to walk up her driveway.

"Hold up," I call out and she spins. "Where the fuck is my goodnight kiss?" Her smile is wide and steals the breath out of my chest. This girl is fucking gorgeous. She's back in front of me, and I reach out to wrap my hand around the side of her neck, bringing her in closer. Our lips brush, and I kiss her softly. "Make sure you remember whose dick had you first today." I kiss her again.

"I'll remember." She blushes and backs away.

So fucking gorgeous.

This next part of my night won't be nearly as enjoyable, but it's time to end things with Faith once and for all. It's been in the works for a while, but we were both clinging on, her for the status of dating one of the four and me because the girl I wanted was just out of reach.

Until now.

BRODY

NINE

My chest is tight and screaming with frustration as I hop her fence, hauling myself up to the balcony. I get to the landing and bend over, gasping for air. I haven't run like that for months and the feeling is euphoric. I needed to get back here before them, or this entire plan would go up in smoke.

But fuck, it was good to watch as she sucked in another one of my brothers, literally. Tonight, everything changes, and I will finally give the monster everything he's been roaring at me for.

I hear Zeke's bike's engine and hurriedly open the window to slip into her house. I cross the hallway and enter her room, eager to watch if Zeke lets me down and decides to come in with her. He doesn't, and I grin as I watch his eyes flick up to her window. Does he see me?

He says something in her ear, his eyes steady on this window, then she backs away, coming up to the house. I hear the front door open and shut, then Zeke shoves his helmet on.

He looks once more in this direction, then takes off down her street. Perfect.

"Cooper?" I hear her call out, and no one answers.

I walk out to the top of the stairs and catch the end of her hair as she disappears into the kitchen. The light turns on, and I know she's reading the letter I left her… From Cooper. I wrote that making my writing as messy as the heathen's.

It's telling her not to worry and that he just went to grab some food. In reality, both of them were called to 'emergencies' and they believe she's safe with Zeke.

Stupid fuckers.

I back up and slip into her father's room just as I hear her tiny footsteps hit the wooden steps. She's humming something, and I can only assume it's because of her post coital bliss. I really need to have a discussion with her regarding her whorish tendencies.

She walks by this room, not even glancing at it, because if she did, she would have seen me just standing just beyond the doorway. No, she's so lost inside her head right now, probably reliving Zeke's pierced cock feeding her eager pussy.

Soon, I will reclaim her, and she'll have to answer to me.

The others will be upset, but they'll have to get over it… Or I'll kill them, whatever happens first. They always knew this day would come, that I would force myself back into her life to rip the answers out of her throat. She needs to finally face what she did to me so long ago.

I hear her shower come on, and I make my way over to her room. It smells slightly like damp grass. I look down and see her discarded clothes from this evening, indeed soaked from the rain. I pick them up and inhale the scent. I smell Zeke, and in her thong, I smell the musk of their fucking. It fills me with a rage so strongly, I snatch my face away from the fabric and snarl. I know I watched them, but a part of me felt disconnected, and I could almost imagine she was someone else. I pocket the panties and drop the rest to the floor.

The monster sinks his claws into my chest and rips. I was too caught up in the anger I felt when I smelled their combined ecstasies that I didn't see the signs of him rousing.

KAILEY-HIMARI

The hot water feels good as it courses down over my back, taking the cold rainwater with it. I'll be lucky if I don't catch a cold after tonight, but I don't care. Every single thing was worth it. With Zeke, I felt another piece of my heart notch back into place, and I'm almost whole. *Almost.*

I shouldn't think of him, his dark tousled hair, and those icy blue eyes. I shouldn't care that he's been missing for months, and I definitely shouldn't care about his wellbeing. He never gave one iota of thought to my wellbeing when he set the hounds on me the second my high school career started.

But I do care, I care too fucking much, and the ache in my chest is still prominent. I miss those icy blues and those plush lips. I miss his cruel smirks and hard gazes. I miss Brody.

The shower curtain rips from the rings and the sound of them scattering has me screaming before my eyes even open. I open them and try to blink through the water coating my lashes. My vision is blurry, but I see the outline of a man in a black tracksuit with the hood pulled up over his head.

I scream again and try to get out of the tub. This guy isn't any of mine. Even though I can barely see him, I just know he's not one of them. I can't see his face because the hood covers most, but I see the white shine of his teeth as he bares them at me.

I grab onto the destroyed shower curtain that's hanging by two measly rings and try to hoist myself out of the tub, trying to get away from the hooded figure. His wicked laugh is foreign as he watches me struggle and slip my way out. My anxiety is through the roof, and I can literally feel my heart rattling my chest cavity.

The final two rings holding the curtain snaps, and I tumble the rest of the way out of the tub, landing in a heap on the tiled floor. I try to drag myself up, but my fear is crippling me, and the pain in my lower back is intense.

I feel a tearing pain in my skull as I'm being dragged up by my hair. I scream and reach for the hand ripping my fucking hair out.

"Don't fight me and this will go a lot smoother." His voice sends tendrils of icy terror through my body.

"Brody?" My voice cracks with fear. It's his voice, but at the same time, it isn't. He sounds robotic and devoid of emotion.

He finally lifts me to my feet, and I slip through the water, trying to free myself from his grasp. I turn and we come face-to-face. It's Brody. I can see the sharp cut of his jaw and the determined set of his plump lips, but it's those eyes that make me pause. He's looking at me, but it feels like he's not seeing me, like a fog has descended over him and he's losing a battle with the dense mist.

"Mine," he growls through his teeth, and I watch as his large fist comes barreling into my face.

My scream is stifled by pain and then blackness.

BRODY

TEN

Fuck.

Fuck.

Fuck!

It happened, and all because I was too distracted by *her.* He got out, and now I have to figure out what damage he left in his wake. The first being Kails lying unconscious on my fucking bed. She's sporting an angry purple goose egg on her forehead, and I cringe, knowing my fist did that.

I look down at the pink knuckles on my left hand and curse again. The monster has no understanding of restraint and while he may have gone to extremes to grab her, in his mind she deserved it. He knew what she put me through, what she left me to endure alone, so I can't be too angry with him. No, I'm angry because I need to retrace my steps, but how do I do that with this one here in my bed?

My phone pings a few times with incoming messages and then vibrates with an incoming call. I know who it'll be, and if I don't answer it, he'll just come over here.

I grab my phone and move into the hallway. "Yeah."

"Tell me it was you." Zeke sounds frantic, and it takes every ounce of my self-control not to fucking snap,

"You care now?" I sneer.

"I always did, asshole!"

"Now, now," I taunt him. "If you scream too loud, you might wake her up."

"Thank god," he breathes, and I can hear the stress slowly leave him in that large huff of air. "Did she go with you willingly?"

"Oui." My lie is automatic and undetected.

"What do I tell everyone?"

"Not my problem." I hang up the phone because his voice is wearing thin on my patience.

I re-enter the room to find Kails sitting up in my bed, running her hand over the lump on her head. Thankfully, *he* dressed her in my clothing because I'm sure finding herself naked in my bed would've made things slightly worse.

Her eyes snap to mine and widen. Her breathing speeds up and her hands fist into the blanket.

"Brody." Her voice is hoarse. "Why?"

I stroll to the side of the bed and sit down beside her. Her body is tense, filled with fear, and I breathe it in deep. It's always been my favorite scent of hers.

"Why, Brody?" she asks again, her voice stronger and

surer.

That fucking bothers me, so I reach out and grab her jaw in my hand, yanking her face forward into mine.

"I told you before I left." I shrug and grin. "I'm going to kill you."

"You're going to kill me, Brody?" I watch her pulse beat rapidly against the pale skin of her throat. "Why didn't you do that at my house, then?"

"Too much evidence to clean up." I release her face and get off the bed. "First, there are a few things we need to sort out."

"Like?" Her voice is still soft, but the fear is slowly leaving her. Can't have that.

I grab her matted and damp hair, slamming her into the headboard. Then I grab the chains I have hanging down the back. Caine and I installed them the same month, just a week apart. I cuff her right hand and laugh when she tries to fight, screaming my name in anguish. I get her other hand in the cuff and step back to watch her struggle for a while.

The way her body moves and the sheen of sweat coating it makes my cock painfully hard. I yank the hoodie off and throw it on the floor, watching her finally settle down.

"Brody?" Ah, there it is. Potent and pure… Her fear. If only she knew how scared I was when she left me.

I reach into my pocket and pull out her panties. I let them hang on my finger and hold it up in front of my face. It's not even under my nose and I can still smell the scent of their fucking. I growl deep and long, holding him back with my anger. He won't get out again so easily.

"Why do you have those?" Her voice shakes as she cries.

"A reminder to myself... The cost of betrayal."

"What?" She looks confused, but I'm distracted by the tears rolling down her cheeks. Tears that Zeke tasted while she gagged on his cock.

I yank the blanket off her body and watch as her legs shake. I know she has nothing on under my t-shirt, and the monster inside rumbles at the sight of her. He wants her as much as he hates her, and his emotions are bleeding into mine. I can't tell who's feeling what.

"Brody." She's sobbing as she realizes my intentions. "Don't do this. Don't ruin us."

The monster roars loudly inside, and I have to cover my ears to keep from letting the sound take over. How dare she ask me not to ruin us?

"Funny, that," I mumble as I control the tremors of anger. "You already did that, didn't you?"

"I told you why, Brody!" she shrills as I grab her ankles.

I tug her down the bed so her arms are lifted taut over her head. She's kicking her feet and screaming. I can't have none of this. So I grab both of her ankles in one hand and undo the belt around my waist. I pull it out and wrap it around her ankles, pulling it tight.

"Brody, stop." Her voice is small and her words short from trying to catch her breath. "Don't be like him."

I still at her words and hold her ankles hostage with my belt in my hand. "Like whom?"

"Justin."

His name coming out of her mouth drives my anger, wiping my mind clear of all coherent thoughts. I flip her over and feel the monster press against my skin. Her arms are now crossed at her wrists, and they look strained, painful even, but I hold him inside and shake my head. He can't have her.

"Oh god," she sobs and shoves her face against the headboard.

Her shoulder blades are bunched together, and her back is arched beautifully. Good thing she was always a flexible girl. I remember watching her dance and wishing I could learn to dance as well, if only to spend more time together. The monster creeps along my mind, his claws scraping against my skin as he suggests a different type of dance. I'm lost in the images he shows us, the need he feels somehow bleeding through me.

While still holding her ankles, I let my pants drop to the floor and watch as they pool around my bare feet. When did I take my socks off? Was I even wearing any? I wiggle my toes and frown at their frigid temperature. Then I shake my head to clear it of any distractions, focusing back on the girl writhing in my bed.

I stroke my cock once, twice, then give the head a hard squeeze as the monster growls. This is what we've been waiting for. I push her ankles until she's propped up on her knees, and she lets out a sob with a low whine.

"You should want this." My voice is hoarse, a deep timber as the monster's mind melds with mine. "You've become quite the whore."

"You hated me, Brody," she sobs around her words.

"I've watched you fuck just about everyone, Kails. Just like the slut we knew you always were."

She's whining about something or other as I crawl up the bed and kneel behind her. Her ass is firm and round, pointed straight up at me. I run my finger through her slit and find her dry. It makes me want to rage and slap the shit out of the soft skin that coats this pristine ass. Make it shine a nice red hue.

With one second of hesitation, the monster roars, blanking my mind. He slips so carefully beyond my defenses, and I watch as I spit into my hand and rub it along my cock. I'm not blacking out this time, but I'm not in complete control either. We've somehow blended and my actions are his. I could fight it, shove him back, but I can't help being curious.

"I would suggest not fighting me." I spread her wide and spit down onto her pussy. At least I'm wetting her. "I like it when a girl has fight."

"Just like your brother," she snarls, then looks at me over her shoulder.

Her red-rimmed eyes and the snot dripping nose make me grin as I slam myself inside of her. There's resistance. My saliva does little for lubrication, and her scream of pain shouldn't be the sweetest melody to grace my ears. Her screaming sobs shake her body, and the motion has her grinding on my cock with perfect pressure.

The monster erupts with a loud groan, the feel of her like euphoria to him. She's wrapped around me like a vise as I pull out and work my way back in. Her pussy tightens, and she screams again.

"Hurts?" I ask as I withdraw and thrust back in.

She doesn't answer, but the wetness coating my cock is astounding. This time when I thrust back in, her sob ends on a soft moan. I don't want her enjoying this, and it angers me. We wanted her to suffer, right? His answering roar has me gritting my teeth, molars clashing, and saliva pooling. *Hold it together.*

My hands grasping her ass cheeks tighten, and I know the hold is bruising. She screams with pain again, and the monster continues his onslaught. I unclench one hand and crack it against her bruised ass once, then twice, only to hit it a third time. I grin at the sound of her sobs renewed and hum at the mottled red-blue of her ass.

Her hands are fisted and crossed, pressing into the headboard. With every thrust, they bounce, and I hope they'll have nice welts too. All branded by me, all swollen because of me, and her pathetic despair… My gift. She'll feel exactly how I did when she threw me away.

When her cries die down, I feel the rush of pleasure. I lose myself in the feeling and force the monster back to pull out just in time. I watch as the squirts of cum decorate her back, then congratulate myself for my control. I never want my cum mixed with the others'.

I get off the bed and head into my bathroom.

"You're just leaving me here like this?" she screams after me. "You rape me and leave me here?"

"Shut up, whore," I call over my shoulder. "I felt how wet you were. You fucking enjoy any dick in you."

I slam the bathroom door and hum along to the sounds of her cries.

desecrated ESSENCE
ZEKE

ELEVEN

"Glad you could come by." His smile is eerie, and his hair is dripping water onto his black shirt. "But now's not a good time."

"I need to know that she's okay." I stick my foot in the door and cross my arms over my chest.

Brody's bigger than me, sure, but I would put up a good fight and he knows it.

"She's fine." He exhales. "We spent the night talking, and she's sleeping in my bed."

I run my hand over my face and shake my head. "I had to tell the others you're back."

"Obviously." He shrugs.

"They know she's here with you, but they won't let her stay long. They will come looking for her."

"What if she decides to stay here with me though?" His

grin is sinister as he's kicking my leg out of the doorway, then slamming the large wooden slab in my face.

I'd bang on the door and demand he open it if I knew it would work, but out of all of us, I know this fucker the best. He would relish in the sounds of my distress and listen to it like it was a piece from a symphony orchestra.

I back away and look up at the second floor. All curtains are pulled tight, and I exhale a heavy sigh. Brody always was her first pick when we were kids. He was her hero and best friend all wrapped up in a handsome package.

I get on my bike and fly down his large driveway, hitting sixty in seconds. If she really has chosen him over us, then the guys and I need to accept it and try to move on. It'll be hard to see them together, but it's her choice in the end.

To think, I just broke up with Faith too. It's a foul thing to think that way, I know, but I'm used to getting regular pussy. I need some kind of outlet or else my past creeps back into my consciousness. Breaking up with Faith was the right thing to do. I shouldn't have cheated on her, and I should've done it right after kissing Kailey the first time. Again, I was just thinking about my constant need to bury the thoughts that threaten to incinerate me from the inside out.

None of us four have had an amazing childhood, but each of us has handled it differently. Caine became dark and broody, answering with his fists more often than his words. Cooper became the center of attention, needing recognition to assuage his loneliness. Brody lost the battle with his mind, succumbing to the shadows surrounding him. And me? Well, I trained my brain like a weak muscle, constantly working it out and toning it to perfection. It's my deadliest weapon. I did it because I needed it to work for me and not against me. Not replaying every rough moment of my childhood.

I pull into the guidance counselor's bungalow where we all have been congregating since finding Kailey missing. It looks like everyone is still here waiting for me to bring back the news. After we found out Kailey left with Brody willingly, the guys and I tried to piece together everything.

Her shower curtain in the bathroom was missing and the rings that held it were resting beside the sink. I thought that was a sign of a struggle until Oliver said she hated the color and kept talking about replacing it. The wet clothing on her floor… That was harder because I had to admit to them what we did in the rain. Then there was the fact that she hadn't taken her phone or purse. Cooper chalked it up to being surprised to see Brody and forgetting them.

Caine has been the most skeptical. His mind sees a crime scene regardless, and it's all because of those mysteries he reads. I have to go in there and tell them that their girl—*our girl*—is sleeping in Brody's bed. Yeah, I didn't miss it when he said it, and it's etched in my brain along with the smug look he wore while those words came out of his mouth.

"So?"

I look up to see Caine leaning against a tree on Oliver's lawn while smoking a joint. He's the one I'm the most nervous about relaying the information to. He can be unpredictable and has had it out for Brody for a while now.

"She's there." I pull my helmet off and hang it on the bike. "In his bed."

Might as well rip the Band-Aid off.

"Huh." He inhales, and I watch as a plume of smoke escapes his mouth, twirling toward the sky. "You speak to her?"

"No." I shake my head. "She was sleeping."

He stretches out his arm, offering me the chance to let

my mind relax, and I can't find any reason to refuse. I take a hit and release the acrid smoke in rings toward the sky.

"I don't get how you're accepting this so well," he states. "You were always one to see the worst in everything."

"Nah, that was Brody. I see reality," I explain.

"Still, man, why does this feel all wrong?"

"Because you love her, and you fear you're losing her?" I offer.

Caine has abandonment issues and has never really bonded with anyone other than us because of it. His father—like the rest of ours—cheated on his mother and transformed her body into his punching bag. While all our parents show a united front to the public, his father left them when he was young. It fucked him up. Then Caine and his mother moved here, and his father started showing back up again. He needed an heir to take over the business he'd started, and Caine was his only choice.

His hatred was buried down deep while he pretended to enjoy seeing his father again, then he learned everything he could about the team his father had put together. In a few short years, Caine began recruiting his own with loyalty to him alone. Now, if there's someone in need of dying, Caine is the man to make it happen.

"She's not going anywhere." It's not a statement, it's a threat.

"It's her choice, you know how she used to feel about Brody." I pull on the joint and hand it back.

"I know how she feels about me now, and I guarantee she wouldn't leave us willingly." I watch him inhale deeply and exhale, the smoke climbing around his head like a storm cloud. "I'm giving her a day. If she hasn't contacted us, I'm going over there."

I fucking know he doesn't mean alone, and I feel a pang in my chest for my brother. Not for Caine, but for Brody.

The others take the news solemnly, and if my heart could sympathize properly, it would do it for Cooper. The guy looks a mess, and I know it's because Kailey is literally his everything.

"She's choosing him over us," he says into his hands.

"We don't know that," Oliver's steady voice says from across the room. I watch him sip his bourbon from a crystal tumbler. Pricey for a guidance counselor's salary. "We need to let her figure it out, though."

"So you're giving up?" Cooper asks as he lifts his head. His eyes are rimmed in red, and the bags underneath could rival my plush pillows.

"Didn't say that." Oliver smiles, and I can't explain the feeling I get when I see a glint of excitement in his eyes.

It looks like Kailey rounded herself up a bunch of psychotic misfits, and the guidance counselor may just top us all. I know what family he comes from, and they rival our fathers' empire, but what we don't know is who exactly Oliver Ballon is.

"He didn't want her before, so why now?" Cooper moans, throwing back the amber liquid in his own tumbler.

Cooper wears his heart on his sleeve, even though it's been broken many times, but not from females. Cooper's father is an addict of all things that can be addictive. Money, power, drugs, alcohol, and pussy. His mother likes to bury herself in mountains of coke and forget she has children or the responsibility of raising them. Jeanine, Cooper's older sister, refuses to come home and has turned her back on her family. Not that any of us blame her, but she broke her brother's heart.

"She has a day," Caine reiterates, keeping his eyes locked on mine.

I hear you, brother. Loud and clear.

KAILEY HIMARI

TWELVE

Have you ever pressed your face into the earth and breathed in its scent? I have, unwillingly of course, and I think that particular fragrance will always be ingrained in my mind. Sometimes, it's the first thing I smell when I wake in the morning, or when I wake up from a nightmare in the middle of the night, and the aroma is pungent in the room around me.

It's obvious why I'm lying here in this bed smelling it now. I sit up quickly and look around me. I'm still in Brody's bed, but he's released my wrists and wrapped me up in a blanket. The chill I'm feeling has nothing to do with the temperature of the room. It's the lingering nightmare still replaying in the background of my mind.

"Fuck, I love it when they beg."

I can still hear Justin's voice like he's right here in this room, and I let a sob escape me when I realize I'm utterly alone here and at the mercy of a monster. Another monster, sharing the same blood as the first who defiled me, and that thought has me shaking in terror. I need to get out of here if I want to survive, and I do. I want to survive for *them*.

I get out of bed and gasp when the pain between my legs intensifies. It hurts, but nothing like the first time I was violated, and it feels something akin to a rough night with Caine. It's bearable.

I pad over to the window and open the curtains, they're some kind of heavy velour material. I look out and see the driveway as the sky twinkles with stars overhead. I don't know what day it is, or what time of night, but I know I can't get out through this window, so I drop the curtain back into place.

"You know…" The sound of his voice has me screaming as I turn quickly toward it. "You talk in your sleep."

"Get away from me." I scramble toward the door and try to turn the handle. It doesn't budge.

"Locked." He pulls out a key hanging from a string around his neck. "This is the only way out. You see, my parents used to lock me in here the very same way."

"Let me go, Brody," I beg him.

"My brothers are willing to start a war for you," he states, completely disregarding my plea. "What do you think of that?"

"They love me," I whisper into the silence between us. "So does Oliver."

"Ah, yes. The Teacher." He grins, the ice of his eyes shining bright in the dark room. "But is he what he says he is?"

"Yes, Brody. He is."

"We'll see." He shrugs and nods back toward the bed. "You should sleep. Tomorrow is a new day."

"I don't want to sleep with you in here," I tell him,

standing firm in my place by the door.

"You either sleep with me in here or in you." He drops the key back inside of his sweater. "Choose."

I know he means what he says, so I slowly get back into bed and lie there looking at the dark ceiling. Sleep is impossible, especially after the nightmare, both in my subconscious and currently sitting in this room. I turn one way, and then after a few minutes, I turn to my other side. I can still smell what he did to me on these sheets, and I cover my mouth to stifle the sounds of my despair.

"Can't sleep?" His taunting voice fills the room. "I'll tell you a story."

I want to tell him to shut up and leave the room, but I know it'll do nothing. I lie still and wait for him to continue.

"That night, five years ago, on this very property. You know the night." Of course, I do. The Landry boys have a penchant for raping girls. "I chased after the girl who meant so much to me, only to learn she wasn't who she said she was. I still couldn't believe it, even when she turned her back and cast me into the frigid cold."

I close my eyes to brace myself for the onslaught of his words. If I'm being honest with myself, I want to hear them and what he has to say for his actions over the years.

"After your mother's funeral, when you wouldn't spare me a glance, I grieved alone. I grieved for the woman who was more my mother than my own and for her daughter who died with her." He takes a deep breath, sounding as if his own words are boring the fuck out of him.

"My first genuine memory of Sara Richard was when I was four years old. I came to your house looking for you when she noticed the fingerprint bruises on my arms. She took me inside the house and made me hot chocolate, then she told me a story. I can't really remember it in detail, but some of it has stuck with me to this very day. She said that every time a child was conceived, it was like a bolt of lightning sent straight from God. She said parents knew when their baby was coming because they could hear the thunder first. Maybe mine weren't paying attention… Because there's no stopping the lightning if you don't hear the thunder."

I know this story well. It was one she told me to make me feel special, and the sounds of her words make the grief I thought long gone surge back up.

"It was then I realized my parents didn't want me, and your mother told me she would be there for me whenever I needed it. That night, I went home and threw a tantrum. I kicked over a family heirloom—some dusty old vase—and my mother lost it. After my nanny tucked me into bed, she came into my room and covered my face with a pillow. I will never know what made her change her mind at the last minute. Bet you wish she didn't, huh?"

I don't answer him because I don't know the answer. The most obvious would be yes, considering what he's done to me, but it's not. It's not a no, though.

"Tell me, Kailey." He stands from the chair and makes his way over to the bed. "What made you run from me that night?"

His hands press into the plush mattress, and his devastatingly gorgeous face hovers over mine. His dark hair falls forward onto his brow and his plush lips purse with anger. Those eyes, an ice-blue so cold, they freeze my heart in my chest.

"You were with Georgina," I whisper.

"So?" He leans closer. "You saw us together before."

"Not like that, not in bed, and not with your clothes off."

"Like this?" He rips his sweater over his head like it's on fire, and I watch the key to my freedom swing against his chest. His hard, muscled chest, with a dusting of hair down the center. He leans back down, the key swinging in front of my face, taunting me with its metal gleam. "She was naked too, though, wasn't she?" His voice is raspy and deep.

I swallow hard, and his eyes zero in on the movement. I've just shown the wolf how scared I really am, and I watch as his large, white teeth flash with pleasure.

He yanks the blanket off my body, and I scream as the cool air hits my skin. His chuckle sends a chill through me, and I realize Brody likes his women scared, just like Justin. His hand lands on my thigh, and I try to scramble up the headboard into a sitting position.

"Brody." I try to get out from under his grip. "No."

His deep chuckle fills my stomach with burning acid, and I try once more to pull away.

"You really think you have a choice? Even after earlier?" His voice is off, the timbre slightly deeper and harsher.

"Brody…" I don't get to finish my sentence as the grip on my thigh intensifies, and he drags me back down the bed.

He's on top of me and his hand locks my sore wrists above my head.

"Tell me how much you hated what I did to you," he growls into my face, his spit landing on my cheek.

"Which time?" I look him in the eye with courage I don't really feel.

The smile he flashes me could melt any girl's heart, but it's hard to feel that when he has me locked under him. His other hand snakes between us, and he lifts his shirt up my thighs, then over my stomach. I have no panties on, and my back still has his cum crusted on it from earlier. His fingers find my center, and I whimper as pain blooms brighter at his touch.

"The last time I was in here…" His two fingers push inside me, and the burning sensation turns into something close to stabbing needles.

"Stop." I try to pull myself away from him, but his grip on me is firm. I feel my tears fall from the corners of my eyes and slide down my temples into my hair.

"You said I was exactly like my brother. Tell me what he did to you, in detail." He ignores my interruption as he thrusts his fingers back inside me.

"Not until you stop."

"I wasn't giving you a choice." He adds another finger, and I cry out from the stretching of my sore opening. "How did he do it? How did he lure you away?"

His fingers pull out of me, and I sob at the relief. "He saw I was upset and asked me if I wanted to talk."

His hand, the one that was just inside of me, clamps down on top of my mound, and he squeezes it to the point of pain.

"You followed my brother to talk?" He looks livid… Incredulously livid. "Kails, start telling the fucking truth." His hand doesn't let up, and I cry out as the pain intensifies.

"I am!" I scream as I look up at the ceiling. "I ran out of the pool house, away from you, and away from all those eyes, watching me with pity. I found them, and it was the perfect escape from you too."

"Them?" His fingers loosen, but I can feel their imprint

still as my flesh throbs from the assault.

"Justin and Lance."

"You followed both guys to talk?" I can't look away from his frigid blue orbs, but the hatred shining in them is almost enough to rival the pain he's inflicting with his hands.

"Just your brother, Lance went back up to the house." I shudder as my words bring me back to that night. "Your brother led me into the woods, and I was happy to follow him. I wanted to hide from you and try to forget what I saw you doing with that bitch. I trusted him."

His dark chuckle leaves me feeling bereft, and my stomach drops when his eyes darken. This time, his fingers skim over the flesh of my pussy, and the touch sends tingles throughout my core.

"And then?" His voice is deep and dark.

"We stopped. He turned on me so quickly, and when I tried to back up, I stumbled. I fell and landed on my ass as he laughed at my clumsiness." I sob again as the memories play behind my closed eyelids, and Brody's fingers continue their ministrations. "He was fast, so fucking fast, as he grabbed my hair in one of his hands and threw me face down on to the ground. Then my shorts were down, and I heard Lance there too. Then your brother stole my innocence, and so did Lance."

He hums as I open my eyes, watching himself as his fingers continue to dance over my flesh. I don't know what he's thinking because his face is a perfectly constructed mask designed to attract the flies, only to eat them when they're too close to get away. I watch the key swing back and forth from his neck, my liberation so very close.

"You want this, huh?" His hand pulls back from my pussy and his long fingers wrap around the metal key.

"Of course, I do," I snarl at him.

His mouth curls up at the corners into a menacing grin, and then he lifts the string from around his neck. If he does something stupid like swallow that thing, I will gut him myself to get it out.

He opens his hand and sitting right there on his palm is the key, begging me to grab it. My hands are still trapped above my head, but I buck my body, hoping I knock his hand, and the key drops. After that, I don't know what I will do, but one step at a time.

He laughs at my attempts and once again curls his fingers around the metal. Then that hand is back down between my legs, and I know the confusion is clear on my face.

"Know what happened later that night? After you were so-called raped?" The cool touch of metal is against my pussy, and I gasp. "I found Lance, and he was talking to a group of guys about the drunken girl that begged to suck his dick out back."

"I begged him to take his dick out of my ass!" I scream, finding a small pleasure in his shocked reaction before he quickly schools his features.

"I fucked Georgina in the pool house, because Kails, I knew he was talking about you."

"You knew what they did, didn't you?" I spit out. "Georgina told you everything."

He leans down, and I feel his fingers slide into me again, only this time it's combined with the cool metal. "Maybe," he whispers, then fucks me with his fingers and the key.

BRODY

THIRTEEN

I wash the blood off the key and my fingers, then replace it around my neck. It's not a lot of blood, but enough to make me feel a craving to see more. Or is that the monster's desire? I shake my head, trying to grasp at reality.

I don't have much time before the guys get here looking for her, so I have two choices. One: she calls them and tells them herself that she's here working shit out with me. Or two: we leave and go somewhere else. If I go with option number two, it throws a wrench into my plan, and right now everything is planned perfectly.

I walk back into the room to find Kails still softly crying in the bed. All she does is cry; she has never been like this before. The Kailey I knew was strong and stubborn, never backing down from a fight. Maybe my high school terror changed her. I can't help but feel a little pride in that.

"You need a shower," I tell her, crinkling my nose to

drive my point home. "I'll get you some food and water while you do that."

At the mention of food, her stomach growls loudly, and she clutches it with a grimace. Sometimes I forget the necessities needed to stay alive, such as food and water. My brain works on another frequency, so I only eat or drink when I feel the pain of needing them. Or the monster reminds me with his loud roars.

I leave the room, locking it tight. There's no way for her to escape from that room, and I took every object out of there that could aid in her self-harm. I know Kails, though. She was never one to harm herself. She just lets everyone around her do it, and if my brother and Lance did have their way with her, then she needs to learn how to fight back.

I don't want someone weak in my corner, not when I have big plans to take over this empire the guys and I are working so hard to get. The monster inside me hums his approval, and I grin, knowing I need to make her tougher. By any means possible.

I get to the kitchen and find some of those frozen waffle atrocities, popping two in the toaster. Kails used to love these with jam when we were kids and milk on the side. I'll make her this, and if she doesn't like it... Well, she can starve. I know the human body doesn't let you go too long without eating, especially if there's some form of food in front of you. At six years old, I found that out, but with dog food. When you're starving, you'll eat just about anything, and dog food is basically a canned meatloaf.

The waffles finish toasting, and I slather them in jam, pour a glass of milk, then head back to the room. I swear if she hasn't gotten herself into that shower, I will drag her by the hair and throw her in there myself.

I open the door and am pleasantly surprised to hear the shower running. I set down her plate and lean against the door, listening to the water hit the tiled floor.

I can just imagine her shampooing that long, thick hair, the foam sliding down her forehead. I imagine her using the bodywash with broad circles to scrub it into her skin, and then I imagine her hand guiding the cloth lower, washing her little, pink pussy.

My cock strains against my pants, and I frown as I realize just how hard I am. Has anything made me this hard before? Yes, watching Kails fuck the guys did as well. I feel him and his need pressing tight against the barrier of my mind, forging his emotions with mine once again. I'm not one to deny myself what I crave, and I feel like I've done that too many times over the last few months. So I'll take what I want now, whenever I fucking want it.

I open the door and enter the steamy bathroom. The mist carries the scent of my shampoo and that alone almost makes me come. I grip my cock through my pants and squeeze hard. I'm in control. It's at that precise moment I hear her soft cries and decide her toughening up needs to be taken up a notch. I shed my clothing and kick them aside. I look down and see my angry swollen cock, begging for release, and I grin.

I slide open the door, and she turns toward the sound with a gasp. She gives me a once-over and shakes her head. "Brody, don't. You've already ruined everything," she says weakly as she continues to shake her head.

"No, you did that the day you turned your back on me," I growl at her, closing the shower door behind me. "You'll spend the rest of your life regretting it."

"You can't hold me hostage forever." Her brows crash together in anger. "And now you're going to keep me alive?"

"I didn't say how long that life would be, did I?" I grin at her and watch as her eyes heat. She wants me, I can see it. She can keep denying it all she wants. "You're not a hostage. You will understand that after today." I crowd into her space and back her up against the wall. She trembles, and I watch as her skin erupts with goose bumps. "Turn around," I demand.

"No." She shakes her head. "If you want to force me, then that's on you, but I won't be complicit."

I grab her arm and whip her around, pushing her face into the hard, unforgiving wall of the shower. Her cheek hollows out under my hand as I push a little harder. She whimpers when I kick apart her legs and step between them.

My heart is pounding with anger, and I feel the monster inside, coursing with a hunger more potent than my own.

KAILEY HIMARI

FOURTEEN

My cheek is smashed against the tile, and I know there will be a bruise there afterward. It can join the myriads of others all over my body and inside it as well. Brody's brutal treatment of me is gradually getting worse, and I'm fearing he may actually kill me when he's through.

The hand holding my face is trembling with his anger. I'm scared of him, and I can feel my heart wanting to crash out of my chest, but I'm not going to let myself continue to be the victim. I'm not helpless, and somewhere inside Brody is the boy that used to be my very best friend. The one who kissed my scrapes and bruises, cuddled me during scary movies, and promised me he would always be with me.

He's broken a few promises along the way, but I know in his heart there's a part carved out for me. I have to believe that he will see me and know what he's doing is wrong. I have to break through to him, even if it really does kill me.

I feel his cock brushing my ass as he kicks my legs apart.

He's hard and throbbing, but I can feel the anger in him rolling over us in waves. He's not himself when he's like this, and I'm beginning to fear there are things about Brody I don't understand.

His hand leaves my face and moves to my ass as he spreads me open to push himself inside me. The pain feels like a butcher knife, working its way into my vagina, and I can't help but scream. I'm sore, swollen, and before I came into the shower, I found blood on my thighs.

I struggle, I try to buck away, and I try to push him off of me but he's strong. He stands firm behind me, forcing his way in until my ass meets his pelvis. I continue to scream as the pain flares and burns hot. He pulls out and thrusts back in as I continue to buck against him. It's not helping me though. If anything, he's enjoying himself even more, so I press my face into the tiles with defeat.

"All done?" He snickers behind me.

I don't answer him, becoming like putty, my body loose. If it's a fight he wants… I refuse to give it to him. I clench my teeth and force myself not to cry out when it feels like my insides are ripping open, when the water stains pink at my feet.

He thrusts in again and stops. I feel his accelerated breathing, the pounding of his heart against my back, and the throb of his cock inside me.

"All done?" I look at him over my shoulder, mocking him.

His eyes narrow and his hands tighten on my waist. I can already feel the bruises forming beneath each pad, but I refuse to cry out. I won't let him know just how painful all of this is on my body and my heart.

When I refuse to look away from his glare, he pulls out of me and turns into the shower's spray. His cock still standing, hard and angry, as he scrubs the water down his face. I'm still pressed against the tile, willing my body to relax, and hoping the pain recedes. This man used to be the boy I loved, and with every minute we're together, I'm questioning where the fuck he went.

"We need to talk, and I have something to show you." His voice sounds nonchalant, like he didn't just fucking rape me moments ago.

"Let me just clean this blood up and I'll be right out. Not like there's anywhere else for me to go, right?"

I turn around and press my back into the cold tile. I cross my arms over my chest, trying to give myself some semblance of modesty. I watch as he turns to look at me, water running in rivulets down his face. A face that looks carved from stone, a beautiful stone with no imperfections and lacking all warmth.

"Right." His eyes give me a once-over and then his guarded expression meets mine. "I used to love you, Kails." So softly, his voice sounds velvety smooth. "I don't know what I'm capable of now, but I used to love you."

Then I watch as he steps out of the shower and closes the door behind him. I used to love him, too.

After my shower, I step out to find a set of folded clothes on the counter. When I pull them open, I see my clothes from my closet, and my heart races at the thought that he snuck back into my house to get them. I need to find out how he was getting past Zeke's top of the line security system, and then I need to fire Zeke as my security company.

As my stomach rumbles again, I cringe and get dressed. I

don't even know when the last time I ate was. It's nearing evening now, which means I've been here almost a whole day, and I hadn't eaten since before my shift at the restaurant.

When I enter the bedroom, I see a plate of waffles smothered in jam and a glass of milk. I'm immediately choked up at the sight. This was my favorite breakfast when we were kids, and my mother used to make it for us regularly. Usually on Sundays, when Brody would end up sleeping over because his house was in an uproar.

When I've finished my breakfast and I'm sitting on the bed, Brody comes back in. His face is once again void of any emotion and his blue eyes look dead. He's never been this empty before. During the last few years at school he'd been angry and vengeful, but at least it was something.

"I need you to call Caine and tell him you're fine," he states, his voice as dead as his eyes. "Tell him we are working shit out."

"I won't lie to any of them." I shake my head.

"I figured as much." He rolls his eyes and sighs. Finally, something other than his cold features. "Remember this moment, when I gave you a choice."

My heart rate picks up, and the palms of my hands grow damp. He comes to stand in front of me, holding out his hand. I stare down into it, then look back up to him in confusion.

"You take my hand, or I tie you up." His offer leaves me with no choice, so I take his hand and let him lead me out of the room.

"How did you get into my house?" I ask him as he pulls me to the staircase. This house is just as familiar to me as my own, even after all these years.

"My brother set up the security. How do you think?" He

looks back at me with his brows raised.

"He told you the code?" I ask, astonished by Zeke's behavior.

"Nope. I just know what he secures and what he doesn't."

Vague answer if I ever heard one. I'll just have to question Zeke the next time I see him. He drags me to the basement entrance, and I pull back on his hand. I know what's down there, even if I never set eyes on it. Brody used to tell me in great detail the room down there designed for him after he was beaten too badly for the help to see.

"I told you to remember I gave you a choice," he growls and yanks on me.

As soon as the door opens, a rush of cold air hits us, and I shiver involuntarily. I don't want to go down there into the inky darkness, so I make my feet like lead.

"No, Brody. Please," I beg him. "I'll call them. Just don't leave me down there."

"Leave you down there?" His eyebrow is still firmly raised. "Oh, no. This isn't for you."

Again, he pulls on me, and I have no other choice but to follow him down the wooden steps. I curl into his back, uncaring of how badly he treated me. I'm scared, and I want him to protect me from the sinister feeling that permeates the air.

His chuckle vibrates against my cheek, and I grit my teeth to stop myself from telling him off. I need his protection, not his wrath. My bare feet hit a concrete floor, and I shiver at the cold contact. It's damp down here, and the moisture seeps its way into the soles of my feet. The air smells musty and stagnant due to no ventilation. I cover my nose and mouth with the sleeve of my sweater, letting Brody drag me deeper into the dark abyss.

He stops suddenly, and I hear the clicking of an old style, pull-string light. When the light turns on, I blink away the glare and let my eyes adjust. As they do, I see a man tied to a chair, his head touching his chest and his hair oily with mats.

"Brody." I dig my nails into his arm. "Who is that?"

The man's head slowly rises, and I scream when I see his face. He's gagged, but he's trying to speak, and he struggles in the chair. "Papa!" I shrill, running to him.

Brody's quick though as he grabs the ends of my hair before I can get to Papa. My head snaps back with the force, and I feel the strands being ripped out like nails digging into my scalp.

"Not so fast." His crisp voice sounds with a *tsk*.

"Brody!" I turn on him with a screech. "Why do you have Papa? How long has he been down here?"

"Call them and tell them we are working shit out." I realize why he has my papa here. It's his bargaining chip to ensure I do everything he says, and it's fucking working.

"I will." I nod because what other choice do I have? "Has he eaten? Brody, please take him out of this room. I will do anything you want."

I can hear my father's dispute through the gag in his mouth, and I would guess because he's seen firsthand what Brody is capable of. Brody's expression doesn't change, he looks bored with this whole situation. I mean, why would he really care? He's already taking whatever he wants from me.

He grasps my hand again and reaches up to turn off the light again.

"Brody!" I scream, trying to pull out of his hold. "We can't leave him down here."

He lets out an exaggerated sigh, then turns back around to face me. His eyes rove all over my tear-soaked face as he shakes his head. "You may regret that soon enough."

"What?" He's making no sense, and I want to reach out to shake him.

"Let's get this phone call done, and then I will bring the bastard upstairs," he growls and snaps off the light.

We're plunged into darkness again, and I scramble into his back, my fingers gripping onto his shirt. "Does he need to be in the dark?" I exclaim.

"Yep," he states, yanking me back up the wooden stairs.

BRODY

FIFTEEN

"Ma petite." Caine's voice comes through the phone's speaker, and my eyes roll into the back of my head. "What the fuck is goin' on?"

"Hey." Her voice cracks, making me want to crash my knuckles into her throat. "Brody came to see me, and I came with him to talk about some stuff."

Her voice shakes, and I grit my teeth in annoyance. Caine will see right through this. I clear my throat, and when her eyes fly up to my face, I make sure she sees murder reflected there. I won't think twice about killing her piece of shit father downstairs.

"Why the fuck do you sound like you're crying?" he barks out, and I breathe in deep to calm my insides. I would love nothing more than to beat his face in right now.

"Because, Caine," her voice sounds snooty as she hastily flicks the tears off her cheeks, "I'm trying to work things out with him, and that means explaining all the vile disgusting things his brother did."

She's staring at me with fire in her eyes, and I can't help the hardening of my cock in my pants. That's what I need to see more of, that steel in her spine and fight in her eyes.

"Oh," he exhales, and I can tell by his tone he believes her. "She'll call me every day. You hear that, brother?"

"Oui," I answer begrudgingly.

"Sha?" Cooper's whiney voice fills the room. "I miss you. You'd tell me if that monster was hurting you, right?"

Next time I see him, I'm knocking him out.

"I'm fine, Coop." Her face brightens at the sound of his voice. "I promise."

"I love you," he breathes.

"I love you too," she answers, running her hands through her damp hair.

"Kail." The Teacher's next.

"Hey, Oliver." She grins. I want to knock her out too.

"How long are you planning on staying there?" he questions, and I grit my teeth. *Forever, asshole.* "Christmas is next week, and remember, we have that New Year's ball."

"I'll let you know in the next few days," she answers.

"Okay." He clears his throat. "I love you."

"I love you, Oliver."

As I bite into my cheek, I can taste the blood in my mouth. This shit is fucking annoying.

"Ma petite." Caine's voice is back. "Zeke will come by tomorrow to check up on you and bring you some clothes with your phone."

She won't be getting shit.

"Okay, thank you."

"You will call me. If there is a missed call, I will come there." His voice is filled with unconcealed threats. "I love you."

"I love you," she whispers back, then hangs up the phone.

"There." Her voice is sad. "Are you happy?"

"Never," I answer honestly. "But that'll do."

I pick up my phone and turn to leave the bedroom.

"Can you please bring my papa upstairs?"

"I told you I would." I just didn't say I would make him comfortable. He'll be tied to another chair.

"Brody," she calls out again. "Where's Georgina?"

"That's for another day." I'm fed up with talking, and if I don't leave this room right now, I'll be putting her mouth to better use.

"Why do you have my daughter?" I knew I should've kept the fucking gag in his mouth.

"Do you play chess, Charles? Actually, don't answer. It's clear your intelligence is miniscule at best. Kailey is my queen, and soon she will do all she can to protect her king."

"What?" His stupid looking face screws up in confusion.

"Exactly." I roll my eyes and bring the gag back up to his

mouth. He hasn't even finished his meal, but I can't bring myself to listen to another word.

"I wonder how she'll react when she learns the truth?" I say as I turn to leave the room. "How will she see her papa then?"

I close the door, sealing off his mumbling around the cloth. If there's one thing I hate, it's a fucking traitor, and Charles Richard is a traitor of the worst kind.

ZEKE

SIXTEEN

I'm nervous, fucking knees-weak nervous. It's because I don't know what the fuck I'll be walking into. Cooper, Caine, and Oliver are pissed, and I understand why. Brody keeps switching shit up and sending us on a whirlwind. I need to make sure he's taking his meds.

Then, there's Oliver. Something seems off with him, and I need Brody to help me figure it out. He's a fucking Ballon for fuck's sake. The Ballon's are known to be over the top messy, and love to hold the title of the most brutal mob family.

I walk up the front porch, and the door swings open, showing nothing. The door slams shut behind me as I step inside. I turn quickly and come face-to-face with a fucking lunatic.

"I always wanted a door that did that. Like a haunted house." His voice is off, too deep, too slow.

"Where is she?"

"In my room." He shrugs and starts walking ahead of

me.

"You're taking good care of her, right?" I start the round of questioning. "She's eating?"

"Yeah, yeah." He waves me off as he ascends the stairs.

I don't hear screaming, so that's a plus, right? Unless... Fuck, would he have her gagged? No, I have to believe Brody still loves Kailey, and he wants to do right by her. They just have demons between them needing to be dealt with.

"She's asked me about Georgina," he casually states, and my heart drops to my feet.

"What did you say?"

"I didn't say shit. I'm just warning she might ask you, too." He grins at me once we reach the top of the stairs.

"Fuck," I grumble.

"Agreed." I watch as he unlocks his door and steps aside for me to enter. "I'll give you two some time alone."

I step into the room and hear the toilet flush in the adjoining bathroom. He closes the door behind me and immediately locks it.

She steps out of the bathroom, and I growl at the sight of her. It takes everything in me not to bust through this door and strangle the bastard. She has a bruise on her head, another on her cheek, and I can see she's barely slept.

"Zeke!" Her eyes are wide as she rushes forward, jumping into my arms. "Are you here to get me out? To bring me home? Wait! He has Papa too! Save him!"

"Hold on." I disentangle myself from her clutches and step back. "Let's talk first."

"What?" Her eyes are wide, and the tears are gathering,

ready to spill over her bottom lid. "You're a part of all this?"

"No one is ever a part of anything with Brody. We either know what he's doing and become complicit, or we don't know shit."

"Zeke!" The disappointment in her eyes breaks my heart. "How could you?"

"Because!" I snap and run my hand over my hair. "You broke him, Kailey! You fucking destroyed him, and he mourned for you. He fucking cried for you, and I saw it all." She takes a step back and shakes her head, but I continue on. "You were all he had! His one bright spot to look forward to. The rest of us were just as dark, just as fucked-up, but you, you were the tether that held him back from the pitch black." I stalk toward her. "And you cut it for no good reason."

"His brother—" she starts, but I cut her off.

"His brother!" I scream. "Not him!" Every bit of hatred I felt for her during those few years after she ditched us comes rushing back. She needs to know she destroyed us, that she decimated Brody when she left.

Her chin wobbles, and the tears finally break free of their confines to race down her cheeks. Guilt reflects in the depths of her eyes, and I can only hope she finally sees it.

"The sins of his brother should've never been his to bear," I say, quieter. "You broke him and now it's only right you fix him."

"He's been raping me, Zeke," she whispers, and I close my eyes at the words.

"He's not in his right mind," I explain as anger rises toward Brody. I'll fucking kill him after I shove the entire bottle of his medication down his throat. "I'll make sure he stops."

"Oh, my god." She turns her back and covers her mouth. "This was always going to happen, wasn't it? You were all going to punish me for how I dealt with being attacked by Justin and Lance."

"Maybe if you tried to remember how you once were… How inseparable you were and forgive him that night for what he did with Georgie. Maybe then things would work out the way they should."

"Why does he have my papa, Zeke?" Her voice has taken on a sharp edge of anger, and I can't help but grin.

"Again, I'm only complicit."

"Get out," her whisper is harsh and filled with rage.

"Use the anger and fix him," I insist as I bang on the door. "I brought you some clothes and your phone."

"He won't give me my phone." She turns back to glare at me.

"He will, if you guys fix what's broken between you." I beg her with my eyes as she glares at me.

The lock clicks, and Brody opens the door wide with a grin to match.

"Everything okay here?" His voice is exaggerated with sweetness.

Kailey turns her back again, and I watch as her shoulders shake. She has to toughen up if she plans to be with us, and Brody is the one to help her do it.

I walk out of the room and watch as Brody closes the door, locking it tight.

"Great," he huffs. "You pissed her off more."

"She says you're raping her," I say to him.

"What if I am?" He throws his arms out wide.

I pull back my fist and slam it into his cheek. "I would say stop," I growl. "We want her toughened, and on our side, not reverted to what she was after your piece of shit brother had his way."

He rubs his cheek with a smirk on his face. "Got it."

I don't fucking know if he does indeed 'got it' but I know he can't continue to torture her if he wants their friendship back. I stalk down the stairs and open the front door.

"Ezekiel," he calls out from the top. "Keep the wolves at bay a little longer, would you?"

"They will want her there for the holidays," I tell him and watch as he throws his head back with a laugh.

"Won't happen."

I leave the house and ride to Oliver's. They're waiting to hear every little thing I have to say and to make sure she's safe. I need to spin more lies to convince myself it'll be worth it in the end.

All their vehicles are here when I pull into the drive, and I recite everything I'm going to say over and over in my head. I can prepare for Cooper; he needs to believe his brothers would never fuck with him. Oliver is pretty laid back, but it's Caine who can be unpredictable. This, for him, could go either way. Either he accepts what I say, and lets them work their shit out, or he storms into the fucking place to get back his woman. If he decides on option two, then Brody and I are dead.

I walk into the house and hear nothing. No talking, no shuffle of feet as Cooper paces, and no clink of the decanter to refill Oliver's glass.

"Hello?" I call out.

"In here," Oliver answers from the family room.

I head in there to find him sitting on the couch watching TV, the tumbler firm in his hand and his hair damp from a recent shower.

"Hey," I say as I sit on the couch opposite him.

"So?" he asks as he tips the glass to his mouth, swallowing the entire contents in one gulp.

"What's with all the drinking lately?" I question.

"This time of year is the worst," he grumbles as he gets up for a refill.

"The holidays?" I know this feeling, anyone from a broken home feels the same.

"Yeah. Most wonderful time of the year, right?" He holds his glass up and tips it back again, draining it all.

"Yeah. You have to deal with family shit or something?" Admittedly, I know next to nothing about the guidance counselor himself. I know enough about his family, but him in particular? Nil.

"Something like that." He grins and sips his third refill.

I hear the back door open, and the smell of grilled meat hits my nostrils. My stomach growls in response, and I realize I haven't eaten a damn thing all day. Worrying about Kailey and the visit fucked me up.

"Zeke!" Cooper exclaims as he hurries into the room. "I knew I heard the bike. How is she?"

And it starts. "She's good. She looks tired, but fuck, she's dealing with Brody. We know what that can be like."

"What do you mean by 'dealing'?" Caine growls as he strides in behind Cooper.

"I mean, they are trying to work out every single thing that's happened in the last five years. Her disappearing act, Brody's mental health and what he orchestrated for her high school years."

"She must have some genuine feelings to want to drag all that up and rehash it," Oliver cuts in.

"They've been close since before they could speak," I retort.

"It's true," Cooper sighs as he falls onto the couch beside me. "I'm scared to lose her to him."

"She's not going anywhere, and if I don't get a call tomorrow evening, neither will Brody," Caine grits out. Brody will go six feet under is what he's implying.

"She'll call." I know at this point she would do anything to protect her father.

The room falls silent, and Oliver taps his fingers against the tumbler. "I will be away for the next few days," he states.

"For?" Caine lifts an eyebrow.

"Got some shit to take care of," Oliver answers with a shrug. He seems calm, but his heavy drinking and strained actions speak otherwise.

"During the holidays?" Cooper asks.

"Always during the holidays," Oliver replies.

Is he drunk? I try to get a good look at his face, but where he's standing has very little light and the shadows obscure most of his features. From here, Oliver Ballon looks more like a mobster than a guidance counselor. Again, highlighting the fact that I know truly little about this guy. What about Kailey? What does she know?

What happens during the holidays with the Ballons? I tuck that bit of information away and tell myself to research it later. I know he said he has very little contact with his family, but very little is still some. I need to know what he's up to, and how this could be harmful for Kailey.

Kailey wouldn't even listen to me right now, anyway. I could almost taste her anger earlier... It was that palpable. She wouldn't trust a single thing I said, but I still stand by my actions. She and Brody need to make up, need to fix everything, or else we will all end up at war with each other.

"That's it?" Caine's eyes scrutinize my face. "Looks like you got a lot on your mind."

"I just got her and now she's with Landry," I say, raising an eyebrow at him. "What do you think?"

"Hmm," he hums. "Scared to lose her?"

"I guess. I really don't know what will happen, or if we even had a chance to begin with. How many boyfriends does she really need?" I huff.

"I knew she'd be the one that kept us four together." Cooper nods. "She was that for us when we were kids. So why not now when we're adults?"

"And added another to the mix for balance." Oliver grins, the look condescending and ominous.

"I need to get home." I stand from the couch. "Mom went on a bender last night. I need to make sure she's alive today."

"Rehab again?" Cooper asks.

"Nah, at this point, I'm hoping she falls down the stairs in her drunken stupor."

"I'll walk you out," Caine says, standing as well.

Should be fun. I nod at the others, then lead the way out of the house.

"Is he taking his meds?" Caine asks as we step out of the front door.

"I didn't see him physically take it, but he looks fine." I shrug.

"How long do I let this go on?" His shoulders deflate and he looks miserable.

"I think as long as it takes. If we push or crowd her, she might pick him."

"Brody would never share her; you know this as well as I do. He wouldn't be able to with his condition," he says while crossing his arms over his chest.

He's right, Brody doesn't have the patience or the want to be generous with his girl, and Kailey could become every bit his girl. His capacity for feeling has slowly diminished over the years. He doesn't have the same reactions to things as we do. He's become methodical in his thinking, any emotions he should express and feel are void. Except for anger, he still has that one, and I saw the proof of it on Kailey's face.

"You're the only one he's letting in. Keep an eye on her."

That would make me feel like utter shit if I didn't already see the end plan. I can see where we have the potential to go, all of us.

Even Brody.

BRODY

SEVENTEEN

Kailey's pissed—livid—because Zeke crushed her hopes of escaping my clutches. No matter, anyway. Being angry takes a lot of energy, and I plan on draining her of most of hers. I get to the room and stand outside the door, there's no sobbing or sniffling that I can hear. That's different.

I unlock the door and step inside. Suddenly, there's a flurry of fists in my face, and she lands one good blow to my mouth, causing me to stumble back out into the hallway. Then, with a screech, she flies up to wrap her arms and legs around me, continuing to slap and punch me in the head.

I can't tell you if it hurts. Nope, all I can tell you is that I'm fucking hard, and I'm only getting harder by the second.

"I hate you!" she screams, her fist plowing into my eye. Okay, that one hurt a bit.

My hands grab her ass, and I squeeze them in handfuls. She screams, something unintelligible, scraping her nails down my cheek. I can feel the sting, and I can tell she's broken open the skin. Without thinking, I grab her face in the palm of my hand, and stride back into the bedroom. I know she can't breathe well like this, and my anger is rocketing.

The monster paces, his nails clenching, and his breathing swift. He wants out, and I can barely hold it together to keep him in. Does she not remember what can happen if he's free?

Her hands are still slapping into my face as I throw her down on the bed, landing on top of her. "Fuck you, Brody!" she screams. "Let me go! I hate you!"

I lift my hand off her face and slap it across her cheek. The noise ricochets around the room, and her body stills as her face becomes stricken. "I would calm the fuck down if I were you," I growl at her, and her eyes light up with anger. She's fucking gorgeous like this.

"Get off me," she snarls, bucking her torso, trying to dislodge me. If I weren't so angry, I'd find this humorous.

I wrap my hand around her throat and squeeze. Do I want to kill her? Yes. Do I want to do it right now? No, but she doesn't know that, and I chuckle as she squirms, gripping my arm. When her skin goes from red to a delicate purple and her eyes cry pretty tears, I release her. I run my fingers over the red prints on her throat as she gulps in mouthfuls of air.

"I want to kill you, Kails." I press my cock into her spread legs. "So I wouldn't piss me off too much."

She tries to squirm out from under me, but my weight pressing into her keeps her from moving. Her hazel eyes glare into mine, and those perfect, pouty lips are pulled back against her teeth. Lips that I kissed just a few months ago… Lips I want to kiss again. My thoughts shock me. I'm not much of a kisser, and I do it because chicks like it. Georgie liked it, but I never actually felt the urge to do it. Until the night I watched my brother die, and right now.

I bring my hand to her hair and run my fingers through the waves. Her hair is a mixture of different shades of brown that shine red in the sun. I've always liked her hair even when I hated her. She watches me closely, her body tense as she tries to figure out what I'm doing. I don't even know what I'm doing right now, but my insides feel like they're at war with each other. I want to leave bruises all over her, making her scream and cry, but then I also want to bend down to press my lips to hers.

I do neither, instead pushing myself off of her, and go to close the door, locking it.

"Brody." Her voice is hard. "Please, let Papa go. I will stay and do what you want."

"He's not here for that. Although, it served that purpose."

"Why is he here, then?" she asks as she sits up on the bed.

I hate how she has pants on today. I liked it more when she was just in my shirt and nothing else. Fuck it, she'll do what I want, or I'll make her.

I head into my closet and grab a white shirt. Her skin always looked good in white, and I want to see a lot more of it.

"Here." I throw the shirt at her. "Put this on."

"What?" She looks down at the shirt in confusion.

"Take off what you got on, then change into that. And just that."

She rolls her eyes but takes the shirt into the bathroom with her and shuts the door. I should've demanded she change in front of me, but fuck it, it's nothing I haven't seen these last few days.

When she comes out, she throws her clothing to the side and sits on the bed. My cock hardens right back up, and this time, I want it taken care of.

"Get over here and get on your knees."

"No." She shakes her head, forgetting—again—that she doesn't have a choice.

I undo my belt and the fly, letting my cock spring out of its confines.

"That's fine." I start toward the door, my dick swinging with each step. "I'll get your father in here to watch me make you do it."

"No!"

I turn and look at her over my shoulder, slowly raising my brow. Then, to my satisfaction, she slides off the bed and drops to her knees. I walk back toward her, biting back a groan when she tips her head to look up at me.

"I'll do this but—" she begins, but I cut her off with a barking laugh.

"You think you can negotiate this?"

"I'll do this, but you will tell me things," she finishes.

"You're doing this, regardless." I shrug.

"Yes, but I'll do it without biting it off," she counters with a smirk.

I grab her chin in a tight squeeze, then bend down into her face. "If your teeth even come in contact with my dick, I will knock you the fuck out."

"Fine." Her eyes roll, and I imagine that's what it'll look like when I kill her. "How about I enjoy it?"

"I don't even care," I growl, and pull on her chin, bringing her mouth close to my cock.

Her tongue comes out, and she licks the tip, closing her eyes with a loud moan. My cock jerks and smacks against her mouth. I know she's faking it; this is her proving she can make it worth my while, and she thinks I would enjoy this more because she is.

She's wrong.

The second she opens her mouth, I grab her hair in my right fist and ram my cock into her mouth. She gags, and the squeeze of her throat has my eyes rolling back with pleasure. Now this… This is good. She tries to draw her head back, but I keep her there with a smirk on my face. She hasn't used her teeth yet, and I know she won't for fear of my fist. Shame.

I pull out of her mouth and drop my hand from her hair. Now she's glaring at me, and I chuckle. "I like it when you hate what I'm doing to you." I poke her forehead with my finger. "But I would love to taste those tears like he did."

"You were watching us." She sounds shocked as she tries to get up from the floor.

"I'm not finished." I grab her hair again.

Her hands land on my jean clad thighs, and she tries to push me away. This is how I like her, fighting me, hating me, and fueling my hunger for her misery.

"Forget my threat already? I'm good with *Papa* watching us," I mock her, then watch as the fight leaves her body. "Tell me how much you hate me."

"I don't hate you, Brody." She sounds worn out. "I only wish I did."

"That's pretty pitiful." I snort as I tip her head back.

"Open up." She does as I ask, only this time she keeps her eyes locked on mine. Those hazel orbs looking resigned as she waits for my cock.

I slowly push into her mouth; the warmth of her breath and the wet glide of her tongue feels as close to perfection as I've ever felt. Her plump lips seal around me as I push in farther, hitting the back of her throat. Her eyes still stay on mine as I thrust into her mouth. I'm not rough, and honestly, I'm enjoying this, watching her as she takes my cock.

Her hands resting on my thighs, slowly move behind my legs and up to my ass. Then she's pulling me faster into her mouth, setting a new rhythm. I watch her greedily suck my cock, her eyes trained on mine, and I can't decide if I like it. When I envisioned this, it was with her fighting me, that hatred shining brightly and her tears of pain running down her cheeks.

I don't… I don't fucking like it. I cover her eyes with one hand, then grab her hair with the other. I'm in a hurry to get this over with. I thrust into her mouth, hitting her throat with force, and her gags become music to my ears. Having her like this, the same way she was for Zeke, is like erasing him from inside her and replacing it with me. When I am through with her, she will just know me, and all the others won't exist.

My need to come hits me fast, and I slam into her mouth one more time, invading her throat as I shoot my load. I feel her tears hit my palm, and grin as I lift my hand, bringing the wetness to my mouth. I lick the moisture as I pull out of her, and moan at the salty flavor. Nothing has ever tasted so good before.

Kailey drops to sit on the floor. She looks confused as her fingers brush along her lips.

"Charles Richard is working with someone to bring my family down," I tell her as I do up my pants. "This someone also kept his nose lined in white and his pockets full."

"Who was he working with?" she asks, her eyes meeting mine with disbelief.

"*Is*," I repeat myself. "Who he's working with, Kailey. He's never stopped, even when his ass was sitting in rehab and pretending to make himself better for his only daughter."

"He was making himself better!" she protests as she gets to her feet. "He went to rehab."

"He had visitors, Kails. People that brought him the shit while he was in there, and he took the time to refine his plan." I could show her his detox right now in the next room.

"Okay." She rolls her eyes in disbelief. "What plan was that, Brody?"

"His plan to kill me."

Her face drops, and she backs up toward the bed. "That can't be."

"It is. I'm my father's only heir, after all. If I'm dead, who takes over the business?"

She sits on the bed and slides her fingers into her hair. She looks so beautiful when her heart is breaking. "Who is he working for?" Her voice is low.

"There you go." I snap my fingers at her. "Ask the right questions. He is working with the Ballons."

"Oliver's family?" Her face snaps up.

"Yes, The Teacher's family." I nod.

"The Ballons hate the Landrys and hired my papa to take you out? Out of all the people, they chose him? It makes no sense, Brody," she huffs.

"What if I told you he owed them a lot of money, and with no means to pay it back?"

"Like he owed your family?" she sneers.

"Exactly like he owed my family. Only this time, there was no way to pay it back. So they forced him to do a job."

"Why give him that job?" She crosses her arms, but I can see she's starting to see the possibilities in what I'm saying.

"The Ballons know how close the Landrys and Richards were at one time. They know Charles was someone I once trusted."

"I don't believe he would've done it." She shakes her head.

"Then you don't know your father, Kails," I snarl.

"What does that mean?" Her brows crinkle in confusion.

"He's killed before."

KAILEY HMARI

EIGHTEEN

"He's killed before."

Now I know for sure Brody Landry has lost his mind. Papa killing anyone is just impossible. He's too sweet and caring to endanger a life. I know this, and I won't let Brody Landry tell me any differently.

"I can see you don't believe me. Maybe if you heard it from him?" he asks, a smirk playing around the edges of his mouth.

I give him a once-over and try my hardest to see the boy I once loved. He has to be in there. That boy would never believe this about Papa, and he would never force me into this situation. Can I find him and bring him back?

"He's due for a bathroom break, and he's not doing too well right now, but we can talk to him," he tells me.

"Not doing too well?" I get to my feet. "What did you do, Brody?"

"He's an addict, Kails. He needs a fix or withdrawals are a bitch." He shrugs like it's nothing.

"I want to talk to him," I demand.

"Okay." Brody nods. "I'll freshen him up and bring him in."

I watch him leave, then sink back down on the bed. Is what he's saying true? How caught up did my papa get with debt? I've seen the credit card bills and overdrawn account statements mailed to the house. The guys are paying them off for me, and yet, I can't see him getting in this deep. I know he wouldn't kill anyone, and I think Brody has a problem with seeing reality clearly.

I know Papa abused drugs and alcohol, but he shouldn't be having withdrawals right now since he's been in rehab for over three months. If he is, then I may have to believe Brody for everything else he's said to be true.

About fifteen minutes later, the door unlocks, and Brody drags in my papa. Only, it doesn't look like my papa. His skin is pale and a sickly shade of gray, his eyes barely open. He's not really walking, more like being dragged by Brody, and he's sweating profusely. It looks like Brody was correct. Papa is going through withdrawals.

Brody sits him down in a chair, then comes to stand beside me. I can't take my eyes off my papa's face, but he has a hard time looking into mine.

"Papa?" I say softly, but he still doesn't meet my gaze.

"Charles," Brody's cold voice cuts in. "Your daughter has a few questions."

"Everything he's told you is a lie. We are prisoners here…" A cough wracks his body, and I jump to my feet.

"Everything is a lie, huh?" Brody sneers. "Then please explain to her what's happening to you."

"I have the flu, and you will not get me medical attention." His voice is hoarse, and it sounds like he really is sick, but he has yet to *look* at me.

"He sounds thirsty," I say to Brody.

"He's not. I've been literally drowning him in Gatorade and fluids recommended for patients detoxing." He shakes his head in disgust.

"Papa," I call him again. This time, he raises his head slowly, and the look in his eyes completely crushes me. He looks guilty and incredibly sad. "Tell me."

"You look more and more like her every day," he croaks out as tears run down his cheeks. "It's hard to look at you."

"Because I look like Mama?"

"Yes, you are her spitting image, and it breaks me a little every time I see you," he mutters.

"What's happening to you?" I ask him, and gasp when he growls.

"I'm a fucking junkie, okay?" His voice cracks and breaks as it rises in octaves.

"How were you getting drugs in rehab?" Brody questions him.

"I'm not a bad person," Papa says to me without answering Brody's question. "I just owe people some money."

"I know," I whisper. "I see all the bills coming to the house."

"Being an addict is an expensive business," Brody cuts in.

"Why, Papa? Why are you doing drugs?"

"It's the only time I am free from her," he says with a gut-wrenching sob.

"From whom?" I take a step closer.

"Your mama!" he bellows, and I scream at the ferociousness in his voice.

"What about Mama?" I cry, unable to hold in the dread I feel filling inside me.

He grabs his head and moans as he sways in his seat. "My head is pounding; I need something to take the edge off. Brody, son, do you have an Oxy? Even a bottle of Tylenol."

"I'm not your son," Brody grinds out.

"Papa, why does Mama's face haunt you?" I would love to see her, but over the years, her face has become foggier, and it scares me. I'm forgetting her.

"Listen, Charles." Brody steps forward, grabbing Papa's hair in his fist. He pulls his head up so he has no other choice but to look at me. "Tell her what she wants to know, and I will find you the plethora of drugs stashed in this house."

My papa's eyes wander all over my face, and I watch as his slowly crumbles. "I borrowed a lot of money from Lyle Landry." That's Brody's father. "The dealership was failing, and I was depressed. I began to self-medicate with Lyle's product."

"He has many," Brody sneers, and drops his head. "Which one?"

"First coke, and then it moved on to many others after that," Papa admits, his chest moving at an alarming speed. "Your Mama found out and ordered me to go to rehab or else she would take you away. I approached Lyle for a loan to pay the dealership fees and mortgage. He was more than generous."

It was true, when the Golden Four cornered me in the school bathroom and played that recording, it was all true.

"A cool half mil, right?" Brody says.

"Yes." Papa nods, then groans from the movement. "He lent me five-hundred-thousand dollars, but I had six months to pay it back. I thought I could spruce up the dealership, invest in other things, and I would have the money in no time."

"That didn't happen." Brody chuckles, and Papa pins him with a glare.

"What happened, Papa?" I ask him.

He doesn't answer me, and lets his head hang.

"He instead sniffed or shot up most of that money," Brody answers for him.

"Is that true?"

Before he can confirm or deny, Brody continues, "Then, the payment deadline approaches, and Charles here, didn't have a cent to his name."

Papa groans again and keeps his head firmly against his chest.

"Papa. Tell me what happened."

"They were going to kill you!" He lifts his head and screams, the noise startling me. "They threatened to kill you if I didn't pay. I called and begged Lyle to give me a few more days." The recording I heard.

"Please," I beg him. "Tell me what happened. Everything."

"I had to make a choice." His chest heaves and tears soak his cheeks. "I had to make a choice between you or her."

"Me or who?" I know who he's going to say before he

says it.

"Your mama," his whisper is barely perceived, but I already knew the answer.

"Justin and Lance killed Mama," I say, my voice shaking with despair and something darker.

"Yes." He nods. "I hired them to do so."

Before I can consider my reaction, I'm striding forward and slamming my fist into his cheek. My knuckles immediately ring with pain, but I don't care because the only thing running through my mind is the piece of paper I found a while ago in his study. The life insurance plan under Mama's name, a precise half a million dollars payout.

"You piece of shit!" I screech, going back to hit him again, but Brody's arms wrap around my chest. "Let me go, Brody." I struggle.

"Let him finish, and then I will let you do whatever you want." His mouth is against my temple, and his voice holds so much promise.

"Finish!" I snarl.

"After your mother was killed, your father decided he wanted revenge. So he began by fucking with my father's favorite whore. Only when I really looked into it, I found out he was having an affair way before your mother was killed on his demand."

Papa's body heaves with a sob, and instead of feeling empathy for his pain, I want to watch him bleed for it. "Who was it?" My voice sounds dark with promise.

"Cassy Hebert." Georgina's mother. Brody continues, "It started when we were twelve."

My gut twists, and I am barely keeping it together. The

amount of anger coursing through my body is scary. It's pumping through my veins and lighting up my limbs with fire.

"Let me guess," I snarl and struggle against Brody's arms. "Georgina found out the summer before high school."

Brody's body stills, and I turn my face up to look at him. He still has his mask firmly in place, but I can tell by the rigidity of his pose that he's piecing some things together too.

"She told your brother I was into him, that I would watch him, and that I wanted him. She set me up that night to be in Justin's sights." I feel the rumble in his chest before I hear it release from his mouth. "It was her retaliation."

His icy blues finally connect with mine, and I see the uncertainty swirling there. He's finally seeing the possibility of his brother's actions.

"Cassy was my friend, that's it," Papa moans.

"Shut up!" I scream at him. "Everything that happened to me—to Mama—was all because of you!"

"I protected you." He looks at me like I'm acting belligerent.

"I was raped because of you!" I scream at the top of my lungs. My insides are ablaze, and I can't seem to quench the anger. "Justin and Lance raped me, and I hid it from you because I didn't want you hurting. I suffered in silence while you fucked around and got high!"

"There's more," Brody says quietly as he squeezes me in closer to his body.

"I can't hear anymore," I ground out through my teeth. I already want to kill my papa.

"You have to," he insists. "Shall I tell her, Charles?"

Papa just moans and swings his head back and forth. I hope the withdrawals kill him. No, that's not enough. I hope he suffers a long, torturous death.

"Fine," Brody huffs like he's seriously put out. "Charles here worked with the Ballons on Cassy's recommendation. They agreed to let him if he killed someone, and that someone is me."

"Were you going to kill Brody?" I ask him.

"Yes." He looks up at Brody with something dark in his eyes, nothing like the man I know. "After everything he's done, you should want him dead too."

I can't deny that Brody has done some fucked-up shit, but do I want him dead? It's his arms around me now, it's his breath fanning my hair, and his protection I feel… Not Papa's.

"And that was your initiation into this gang?" I ask incredulously.

"No, it was payback for what they forced me to do," he grits out.

"Forced you?" I look at him in shock. "No one forced you to have a drug problem, no one forced you to cheat on your wife, and no one forced you to kill her to pay your debts." I can't hold back the sadness, and I begin to cry ugly, angry tears.

"Life isn't easy," he spits out, and I struggle in Brody's arms. I want to hit him so fucking bad.

"My life wasn't easy!" I scream back at him. "But you wouldn't know since you were rarely home, and now I know why."

He was probably with Georgina's mother most nights when I was home alone or in a crack house somewhere, and the thought makes me sick to my stomach.

"I had to kill Brody, or he would kill you," Papa mumbles.

"Brody would kill me?" I already know he wants to.

"Only you know I want you dead," Brody says, his mouth still pressed against my temple. Only he could make such a threat sound endearing.

"Who would kill me?" I don't know what his ramblings are about, and if he's even being completely honest.

"The Teacher," Papa says.

"The Teacher?" My stomach pools with acid, and I can feel the burn making its way up my throat.

"Kennedy Ballon's son," Papa says as if I would know who that is.

"Oliver, Kails," Brody whispers into my hair.

No, that's impossible. Oliver loves me. Oliver doesn't have anything to do with his family, and this is just not adding up. They're lying. I try to pull free from Brody's arms, but his hold is firm.

"Oliver would never hurt me," I say with certainty.

"If I'm not killed here by Charles, Oliver will have no choice but to do as they say," Brody says.

"He doesn't work for his family," I argue. "He has nothing to do with them. Y'all are lying." I feel the panic swelling, and my head thumps out a painful rhythm.

"He works very little for them, just enough to be left alone most of the year," Brody explains, and my heart breaks at the words. I don't know why they sound plausible.

"How did I get so mixed up in all this?" I whisper.

"Thank your papa." I feel Brody shrug behind me. "This all started with him."

He's right, it did, and I can't sum up an ounce of love for the strung-out junkie in front of me. He was my everything at one time, and I thought his family was his, but I was wrong.

"I hate you!" I snarl at Papa. "I hate you for me, and I hate you for Mama. She deserved better!"

He cries, and the sound does nothing but make me hate him more. He's weak and disgusting, like I was… Until this very moment. No more though, I'm done with others dictating my life, abusing me and using me. From this moment on, no one owns me, and no one rules my fear. I won't let terror or torment control me; I will avenge Mama, and it starts here.

I break out of Brody's hold—or he lets me go—and I stalk to Papa, my fists clenched tight.

"You're no longer my father." I don't even recognize my voice. "One day, I hope to watch you bleed to death."

He lifts his head, and the shock in his eyes quickly turns to anger.

"Why not today?" Brody says from behind me, and I hear something skate along the floor.

I look down at my feet and see a switchblade. It's dead center between Papa and me, and I watch as he looks down too. It's in one split second that the man I call Papa dives forward for the knife, and in the next split second, he's aiming it at me. His arm is trembling with a frantic look in his eyes.

"Watch me bleed one day?" he spits out as his eyes move quickly between Brody and me. "I made sure you were the one to stay alive. Maybe I picked the wrong person."

Brody's foot appears on my left side and kicks the knife out of my father's hand. The knife arcs up in the air, and Brody's fist slams into the side of his head, making him crumble to the floor. Brody's breathing is harsh and quick as he dives forward to grab my father by his hair. He drags him back up and makes him face me.

"You were thinking about sinking that knife into your pretty little daughter, weren't you?" he says with venom-soaked words.

My father's eyes lift to look into mine, and the look of betrayal is clear. I don't know why he feels betrayed. I worshiped him and loved him through all his hardships. I can't ever forgive him for Mama and the catalyst of his involvement in how my life spiraled.

Brody brings the knife to my father's throat and presses into the skin. I don't know when he grabbed it or how, but he has it, and he's watching me, waiting to see what I want him to do. Is Brody actually letting me decide something? Waiting for my consent to murder my father?

"Maybe you want to do it?" Brody smirks. "I have another knife on my belt here." He chuckles when I gasp at the size of the hunting knife strapped to his belt. "Too big?" he sneers, then throws me the switchblade he had held to my father's throat. "Use that instead."

The switchblade is tossed at my feet, and I jump back at the proximity it lands to my toes. I bend down to pick it up when I hear my father and Brody scuffle. I look up in time to see my father grab the knife from Brody's belt, and as if in slow motion, I watch the blade descend toward Brody's chest.

From then on, things are blurry, but my actions are purely instinctual as I run at my father with the switchblade in my hand, stabbing it into his neck, the skin providing little resistance to my attack. The feeling of wet warmth sliding down my hand breaks me out of my trance, and I watch as my father falls to his knees, his hand coming up to the knife still protruding from his neck.

Brody stands staring down at my father, and I slap my

hands to my face, shocked as I watch him fall face first to the floor. "Oh god..." I moan." Oh god."

Brody steps forward and pulls my hands from my face, transferring wet blood against my cheek. "You just killed your father to protect me." He sounds smug, not at all surprised in the least.

"Oh god." I'm still in a state of shock as I watch the blood pool around my father's head.

"Kailey." His voice is softer, as his hands come up to my cheeks, not caring about the blood smeared across one.

"Brody." My voice catches as I let the weight of my actions hit me full force. "Oh no..."

His forehead falls to mine, and our breaths mingle in the tight space. "Why did you do that?" he asks in a hushed whisper.

"He was going to kill you." My answer is quick and honest. I guess what I really mean is, I would rather see my father die than the possibility of Brody dying.

His mouth inches in closer to mine, and I feel the brush of his lips. The warmth of his body penetrates my skin as he crowds mine. Our torsos meet, and our thighs touch.

"Don't let this change how much you hate me." Every movement of his lips is like a dance against mine.

I dart my tongue out to wet my lower lip and it comes into contact with his. The groan that leaves his mouth is raw and guttural, his fingers clenching into my cheeks.

"What have I done?" I whisper, taking a ragged breath.

"You've just proven how tough you can be." Then his hands leave my face, and he backs up, stealing the warmth he was giving. Brody looks down at my father and shakes his head. "That's going to be a bitch to clean," he mumbles more to himself than to me. "I can't call Cooper out here for this one."

"Cooper?" What the hell is he talking about?

"Yeah. Cooper is the expert at making murders look like accidents and making crime scenes disappear." He shrugs, and a smirk flashes on his mouth. "What? He didn't tell you?"

Crime scene, oh god, I made my papa into a crime scene. My hand flies to my mouth as I try to stifle the groan.

"I'll leave you two alone. I bet you have a farewell you need to say." He backs up toward the door.

"Do not leave me in here with him." I look up at him.

"It's your papa." He raises a brow, clearly thinking this is a game in his demented mind. "I guess that's wrong." His fingers scratch at his chin. "He's not *Papa* anymore, now he's just … dead."

"If you leave me in here, I will pull that knife from his throat and shove it in yours the second you return," I snarl, feeling overwhelming anger for the boy who feels nothing.

He bites into his plump lower lip and grins. "Was that supposed to be intimidating?" I watch as his hand cups around a pronounced lump in his pants. "Because fuck, I think I like it."

"Brody!"

"Fine, shit. Just stop fucking complaining. It's giving me a headache." He taps his temple. "And he hates a headache."

He? Who the fuck is he talking about? I don't waste any time asking and hurry behind him as he leaves the room. Brody walks like time doesn't pass him by. His steps are unhurried, and his swagger is pronounced in his hips and shoulders. He looks completely at ease for someone who was almost stabbed and witnessed a murder. Too at ease.

"Did you plan that?" I ask him. No reaction. "Did you set that up to happen? Did you want me to kill him?"

He stops and opens another door. I know this room because its double doors will forever be ingrained in my mind. This is Brody's parents' room.

"It wasn't exactly what I had in mind, but the outcome was still the same. The piece of shit is dead, and you avenged your mother." Cold words spoken without an ounce of warmth.

"How did you find out, Brody? Did you know it was Lance and Justin before I told you?"

He leads me into the room and shuts the door. I notice this one can't be locked by a key, and again I feel sorrow for the little boy he was.

"When you told me that night … that they killed Sara and raped you, that was the first I heard of both instances." He's quiet, thoughtful. "I did my research, starting with whatever my father had on yours, then lo and behold, I did indeed find the pictures my brother took to verify his kill."

My breath gets lodged in my throat as he describes my mama as just another hit. No emotions for the woman who treated him like he was her own.

"And them raping me?" I ask quietly, hoping I will see even an iota of sympathy in his eyes.

"I'm still trying to work that out. I don't know what to believe. I will admit you showed signs of post trauma, but then you started playing leapfrog on all my boys' dicks. Doesn't make sense." He shakes his head, and I stare at him with my mouth agape.

"I love them," I say in what feels like a shameful confession.

"All three of them? Even Zeke?" His brow is still raised.

"I love Cooper, Caine, and Oliver. I don't know how I feel about Zeke at the moment."

"Zeke believes you were raped by them." He nods. "But Zeke will always choose me over any other person."

"Why?" I ask in confusion. I look down at my hands still covered in blood.

"Because I saved him from certain death sophomore year."

BRODY

NINETEEN

Am I really telling her all of this? Why?

"What do you mean?" she asks as she steps closer. Her hands are still slick with her father's drying blood. It's all over her face and in the thick waves of her hair. I want to lick it off every inch of her face and see if it tastes as good as she does. "Brody?"

"Go wash up, I can't concentrate when you're full of blood," I tell her. "My mother's closet is there. Grab some clothes."

She looks back down to her hands again, and her face slowly begins to tremble. "His blood for hers, right?"

"Oui." I nod and clear my throat. "Yeah."

She lifts the blood-splattered shirt over her head and drops it on the white carpet. Kailey-Himari Richard was always beautiful. That will never change, but right now, standing in front of me, covered in blood and looking savage, she's breathtaking.

Her breasts are perfect handfuls, round and perky. Her stomach is toned and narrow. Her legs are long, and her ass is almost too big for her figure… Almost. She turns on her heel and walks into the bathroom, closing the door behind her. A few seconds later, I hear the shower turn on, and I exhale the breath I was holding. I can't waver for this girl; I need to remember what she did to me, and what she did to us.

I storm out of the room, my anger renewed, and stalk into mine. Her piece of shit father is making a fucking mess with his blood seeping into my fucking wood. I pry my hunting knife out of his cold, stiff hand, then pull out the switchblade lodged in his neck.

With the knife free, I watch as his thickening blood oozes out and splatters to the floor. This man was someone I used to look up to, a father figure I could rely on, and an extension of the family I saw in the girl that stole my heart, then kept it.

I was always enamored by Kailey, but once I was old enough to understand that adults marry and raise families, I deemed her my person. I basically wrapped up my broken, defective heart and placed it in her safekeeping. All these years I've been without it, and as cold as I am, I knew she still kept my only warmth safe.

I just can't forgive her for leaving me in a world where she was my only saving grace. The worst part was that she knew it. She knew my home life was tumultuous. She knew I was suffering at school, and she knew her house was my refuge. Then she took it all away with no explanation and no remorse.

The months after leading into years, I became more and more bitter, and every time I saw her face, I wanted to watch her suffer. Then Zeke almost died, and his road to despising Kailey began.

Zeke was never fully on board with our bullying Kailey

in freshman and sophomore years. He watched but never really participated. Cooper always held a flame for her, so he was easily manipulated through his loss, and Caine is a sadistic fucker who loves to watch anyone suffer.

It was sophomore year that Zeke's self-harm became out of control. He was cutting constantly, slicing into his skin, and staring transfixed by the sight of his blood. I never got why he needed to do it, but I understood the need to watch something bleed. When I asked him why, he explained it was his only outlet for the things he kept inside.

It was a week before summer break, Georgina was throwing another end of school party, and we were all getting intoxicated. Zeke hit the bottle hard that night, and by the sight of his long-sleeved Henley and track pants, I knew his father had laid into him again. This used to be Kailey's expertise. She could draw Zeke out of his head after those episodes and bring him back from the brink of destruction.

But Kailey was gone, and this particular episode was severe. With no one to conciliate the war in his head, we were all left to watch as he slowly descended into the recesses of his depression. Descend, he did. It was a few hours later I found him sprawled on the bathroom floor in a puddle of his own blood. I wrapped his wrists tightly and took him to the hospital in time. Then I paid off the doctors and nurses to keep their mouths shut. No one knows what happened that night except for the two of us.

That night, the last vestiges of my feelings for Kailey evaporated, and I became fully dead inside.

She's sitting on the bed when I return, dressed in my mother's favorite nightgown, and biting on her fingernails. Her large hazel eyes, filled with sorrow, raise to look at mine, and I can't hold back the need to rip that fucking gown off of her.

And why not?

I stride forward and fist my hand into the front of the fabric, pulling her up to stand in front of me. Her body is lax, as if the fight has completely left her, and her head falls back to keep her eyes trained on mine. I flick open the switchblade—still coated in her father's blood—and run it down the gown's silky material. She winces at the sight of his blood, but she doesn't fight me, and that's probably a good thing because at this moment, I wouldn't mind seeing her bleed as well.

The flaps of the shredded material fall open, and Kailey is bared to me. She doesn't fight it, doesn't try to cover herself up, and stands there waiting for what I'll do next.

I press the tip of the blade into her cheek and lightly glide it downward over her lips. A trail of drying blood follows the blade's path, and she sticks the tip of her tongue out to touch the sharp edge.

"What does your father taste like?" I ask her, my voice gruff with arousal.

"Like broken promises and lost dreams." Her voice is soft.

"What do you think you would taste like?" I press the tip of the blade against the skin of her right breast.

"Probably something similar." She continues to watch me. "You should find out."

I don't know what game she's playing, and I don't really care to figure it out because right now, I want the taste of Kailey's blood on my tongue.

I press the knife deeper and hear her whimper as I drag it down. I continue my carving as the blood runs over her nipple, then drips off the end onto the white carpet under our feet. The overwhelming need to taste her has me dipping my head forward and sucking her nipple into my mouth.

Her blood is sweet, and her moans are like a melody I thought I'd never want to hear. I release her nipple—the peak hard and tinged in red—and run my tongue over the cut on her breast. Her flavor bursts inside of my mouth, and I can't help but agree with her. She certainly does taste like broken promises.

My tongue glides up her throat and over her chin, then I'm flicking it against her bottom lip. "Want a taste?" I ask her.

"Yes." Her response is immediate and husky.

Her mouth falls open, and I bend my head down to brush my lips over hers. Then I seal them together and plunge inside her mouth with my tongue. It's eerily similar to the last kiss I had given her in the library at Zeke's house. It's angry, possessive, and all-consuming. I forget the resentment, the hurt and need for revenge. Right now, I just want this girl, and I want her to give me everything.

I will fuck her, and then I will continue with my plan.

She groans into my mouth, and I walk her backward onto the bed. Once the back of her knees hit the mattress, she falls and bounces on her back, her breasts mimicking the movement. Her right breast is still bleeding, and I hover over her, licking some of the blood as it rolls down her rib cage.

She grabs my hair and drags my head up, her eyes watering as she looks at me. "This doesn't change how much I hate you," she says, and once again I'm ravishing her mouth.

No, she doesn't hate me. She only wishes she does. I can't stop the need to taste her, and I want to be inside of her so damn bad. Before I can remove my belt, I feel her small hands working it undone.

We're staring at each other as she pulls open the belt, and she releases the zipper. With the switchblade still firm in my hand, I plunge it into the mattress right beside her head, and chuckle when she screams. That's better. This isn't going to be some happily ever after moment.

I shuck off my jeans, and grin at the shock still registered all over her face. Her body is no longer pliant and willing, she's stiffened up with fear. A scared Kailey is so much better than a willing one. I kneel between her legs, forcing hers to spread wide, and I look down to see her pussy weeping, preparing for my cock.

Her eyes fall as I grab my cock in my hand and pump out a hard, fast rhythm. My body knows it well. This is what I do when I need a fast release so I can think, and right now, I have the best motivation in front of me.

Once the realization hits her, I watch her face morph into anger as she tries to move away from me. I pull the knife out of the bed and lean back over her. One hand continues to stroke my cock, while the other presses the blade against her neck, hard enough that a bead of blood bubbles out and runs down to the bed.

"I bet you wanted this cock pounding inside of you," I say as I watch the blood continue to drip down her neck. "Just when you thought I was coming around or starting to care."

"Get off of me." Her voice shakes with anger and embarrassment.

"Are you sure? You wanted my blood-soaked kisses just a minute ago," I groan as my release comes on.

Her eyes spit fire and her hands fist against my chest as

she tries to push me off, but I'm so close to the end. There's nothing she could do to move me, and I lean forward to lick the next drip of blood. The taste of it, her scent, and my mother's destroyed nightgown, all send me tumbling over. I come all over her lower belly and moan her name.

She's shocked in place on the bed as I lean up and look down at my cum on her belly. It runs down toward her pussy, and I do nothing to stop it. I run two of my fingers through the pool under her belly button, then look up to meet her eyes.

"You're wet for me," I state.

"You're a psychotic asshole," she fumes.

With the knife still in my hand, I fall forward, letting it sink through her hair and back into the mattress. She gasps at the knife's proximity to her face, and I take her moment of confusion to sink my cum-soaked fingers deep inside her.

She's wet, and her pussy clamps around my fingers, eager to suck me in deeper. "Brody!" She stares up at me in shock. "You didn't just do that."

As much as her words are fighting me, her thighs drop open wider, and her pussy is fucking dripping around my hand. I pull out my fingers and thrust them back in. She tries but cannot hold back her moan.

I push my thumb up against her clit and move it in tight circles. I want to see her come just once by my hand. Her face flushes red, and her eyes roll back as I pick up speed. Her hips lift, giving me better access, and I slam my fingers inside of her harder and faster. Her pussy tightens as I feel her orgasm coming, and I push my thumb harder against her clit.

The juices pool around my hand as her head tips back on a scream. The cut on her throat drips faster as her pulse beats against the skin, and I lean forward to swipe my tongue through it.

I pull my fingers out, and she looks at me while her breathing slows back down. My hand is soaked, and I grin at her as I stick the two fingers in my mouth. I taste her and me both, and I slowly drag them back out. When she finally comes to her senses, I watch as the horror of her actions slip over her features, and I laugh as I push off of the bed.

"Your papa is dead in the next room, and you just came the hardest I've ever seen you come before."

She grabs the scraps of fabric, pulls it around her body as she turns on her side and curls up into a ball. She's not sobbing or crying, just lying there looking at the wall in silence.

ZEKE

TWENTY

"We have a problem." His voice betrays nothing over the phone, but I can't control how fast my heart picks up inside my chest.

"What do you mean?" I ask Brody.

"I need you to get over here, and fast."

"Kailey?" I ask.

"She's fine," he huffs. "Just get over here now." He hangs up.

It's late—I look at the time on my phone—just after three in the morning, and I groan as I get out of bed. There's no way I'm ignoring a phone call from Brody, especially one of him stating he needs my help, and Kailey being in the same house.

I pull on a hoodie to cover the few bandages on my arms and hurry out to my motorcycle. It takes me about five minutes to get to Brody's, and I park my bike in a hurry.

All the lights are off, and an ominous feeling comes over me. Nothing about this feels right, and I am in a full-blown panic when I race up his front steps and watch as the front door swings open.

"Where is she?" My words are clipped, and my breathing is erratic.

"Sleeping." He approaches me from behind. "I need your help."

I turn to face him and raise my hands in exasperation. "What could it be now, Brody?"

"Come upstairs. I need you to do that thing you did last time."

Last time… Last time when?

He opens his room door, and I notice this time it's not locked. The door swings open, and the first thing I see on the floor is blood. A lot of blood.

"Where is she?" I scream as I push my way inside.

The room is empty save for the dead body on the floor. A man by the looks of it, and I sag with relief.

"I told you; she's sleeping." His voice is even as he looks from me and back to the body.

"Is that…?" I walk closer to get a better look at the face.

"Mr. Richard himself," Brody says smugly.

"Bro, please tell me you didn't kill her father in front of her." My head drops back on my shoulders as I stare at the ceiling.

"I didn't kill him." I whip my head around to stare at him as he shrugs. "She did."

"You told her."

"She wanted to know everything, so we started with this shithead." He kicks at the body.

Now I know which last time he's referring to. "You want me to dispose of him?"

"Yeah, then I can clean this up."

"It'll take a few hours, so let's get started," I groan.

Four hours later, I am standing outside of his parents' room door, stinking of bonfire and barbeque. I'm bone deep tired, but I need to see her before I leave. The door creaks as it opens, and it takes a minute for my eyes to adjust to the dark. When they do, I don't see Kailey anywhere. I step inside and walk over to the bed. There's a ripped nightgown, a few drops of blood, and what looks like a few locks of her hair.

He assured me she was fine and sleeping in here, but why the fuck did I believe him?

"Bebelle?" The room is empty.

I scan the room for any sign of her when I catch a light on under one door. The soft sound of water falling grows louder as I walk toward it. I open the door and step into a bathroom that can only be described as lavish.

There's a large shower to the right, completely encompassed by glass, and no one under the spray. I open the sliding door and find Kailey sitting in the corner with her head to her knees, her arms wrapped around them.

"Bebelle?" I whisper. Her head pops up, and she laughs,

not one filled with actual mirth. No, this laugh is sending shivers down my spine. I pull up my sleeves and reach in to turn off the water.

"Cutting again, Zeke?" Her voice is condescending as she observes my newest bandages.

"Again?" I sneer back at her. "It never stopped."

She stands up, and then I growl when I see her body. She has bruises that look yellowed with age, maybe from Caine, but it's the carving over her breast and the puncture on her throat that has me pissed.

"I now have a few of my own. How ironic." She laughs again, the slightly maniacal sound piercing my chest.

Her fingers brush over the *BL* on her right breast and then up to the nick in her neck. I turn around and grab an over-the-top plush towel, holding it up for her.

"Why are you here?" she questions as she steps into it.

I wrap her up and grab another for her sodden hair. "Business," I mutter.

"Oh!" She snaps her fingers and grins up at me. "My piece of shit father, right? You smell like fire and roasted Charles."

This isn't Kailey. She adores her father, and I know what the *piece of shit* did, but should she be acting this way? Is there no grief?

"Yes, I helped Brody with the cleanup." I keep watching her face for a sign, any sign of remorse.

"Good." She nods and steps out of the bathroom. "I hope he is restless for eternity in Hell. He killed Mama."

"I know," I breathe.

"Of course, you do." She chuckles and heads into the

closet. "Do you also know I killed him?"

"Yes," I answer honestly.

"But do you know why I did?" She steps back out completely naked, Brody's branding shining a bright red against her olive skin.

"Because he killed your mother?" I think she's losing it here. Maybe this isn't working as Brody promised it would.

"I was livid when I found that out, maybe even murderous, but no." She pulls on a man's shirt, and I watch as it hits her thighs. "I killed him because he tried to kill Brody," she ends on another chuckle.

He didn't tell me that, and I'm fearing Brody is slipping in and out of his consciousness, unsure of what he's doing half the time.

"I'm going to talk to him about letting you come home."

"Aw." She waves her hand dramatically. "Thank you for *asking* him to let me go." Then she punctuates her sarcasm with a roll of her hazel eyes.

"When he told me the plan, it was to strengthen you, to make you aware of everything that's been going on, so you could be with us fully," I try to explain.

"Oh, is that right?" She leans her head to the side. "You really thought Brody would share me with you guys? That him watching us… Was what? Him coming around?"

Her questions stir all the doubt I had free, and I shuffle from foot to foot. "Yes, I thought he would come around. You seem to have that effect on us."

"He never plans to let me go." Her brow rises, and she slowly walks toward me. "Maybe he'll share me with you, though."

"Maybe." Brody's dark voice comes from the doorway. "Maybe I could stand Zeke."

"What's wrong with her?" I turn on him as Kailey's hands encircle my waist from behind.

"I don't know. I've been scrubbing blood all night." He lifts his hands to show the pink stain. Then he steps forward to wrench her hands off of me.

"Guess not." She giggles behind me.

I turn and grab her chin in my hand to get a better look into her eyes. The glossed over irises and pinpoint pupils tell me she's on something, but what? And how much?

"Bebelle, what did you take?"

"Take?" Brody strides forward and roughly pushes me away from her. "What did you get yourself into, Kails? Don't make me force you to vomit. We both know how much I'd enjoy that."

"What does your mother have in here?" I ask him as I make my way into the bathroom.

"Fuck knows," he answers. Mrs. Landry is well known for her love of prescription drugs and alcohol. It's what helps her tune out her family.

I pull open the medicine cabinet and groan when I see the assortment of pill bottles in front of me. "There's no fucking way of knowing!" I yell out.

I hear a scuffle and turn to see Brody dragging a struggling Kailey into the bathroom.

"Guess we have to do a manual stomach pump," he says as he brings her to the toilet.

"I didn't take a lot!" she screams as she tries to pull her

hair out of his hand. "I don't want to die! I need to stay alive to watch you die!"

Brody stops and releases her hair. All the while his jaw is clenched and ticking. "Watch me die?" he asks her.

"Yes!" she screams into his face. "I want you to die!"

I step between them because the look in Brody's eyes can only be described as death incarnate.

"Bebelle, go on back in the bedroom and sleep that shit off." I watch her hurry away, and then turn to face Brody. "Bro, chill." He has a hard time meeting my eyes, and my stomach fills with dread. "You need to take the meds."

"I can't think clearly when I take them." His hands grab onto his hair. "I need to be thinking clearly right now."

"Your rage is too much," I try to explain. "Without them, you become unpredictable and angry. You carved your fucking initials into her chest."

"She loved every second of that." He grins at me. "I made her come afterward too."

I know Brody isn't a liar, and I would believe he could bring Kailey to her knees because of how she felt or still feels about him. I follow him out of the bathroom, and we find bebelle standing by the window, looking up at the sky.

"Where did you burn him?" she asks quietly.

"On Landry land a few acres out," I reply.

"What day is it?" She turns to look at me.

"December twenty-third."

"I want to be with the others for Christmas." She looks at Brody.

"Fine," Brody relents, but I see the evil gleam in his eyes. "Then I'll kill you on New Year's Eve."

"What?" I exclaim, and Kailey just shuts her eyes in defeat.

"Those are my conditions." Brody shrugs.

"Fuck's sake," I breathe and scrub my hand down my face.

"Zeke," Kailey calls out to me. "I forgive you for your part in all of this."

I don't know why her words cause a chasm to split apart my heart, and now I feel like the one bleeding out on Brody's floor. Fuck, Brody, and fuck his possessiveness with our girl. I stalk toward her and take her face in my hands. This woman has always been meant to tear me down and rebuild me.

I sink my teeth into her bottom lip and then suck it into my mouth. His growl sounds from behind me, but like I said, fuck him. I glide my tongue across her mouth, and she opens up for me on a gasp. Then I'm tasting her, sinking into her pool of sweet honey, and nothing will ever taste this exquisite again.

Her hands grab onto my sides, her nails sinking in, and her body moving in closer. My fingers slide into her hair, and I pull her head to the side, angling us so I can thoroughly devour her. She sucks my tongue into her mouth, and I growl, wishing we were alone, wishing I could strip her clothes off.

"I hate to break this up, but I'm feeling fucking murderous this morning."

Kailey pulls away at Brody's words, and I groan at the loss. She turns back to look out of the window, and I realize I'm dismissed. I turn and walk past Brody.

"Another mark on her and I'll murder you myself," I tell

him.

"You keep taking away all my fun," he mocks at my back, but I don't bite the bait.

He knows there are four other guys that will kill for that girl, and those odds aren't in his favor.

KAILEY HIMARI

TWENTY-ONE

The cuts on my chest sting every time I take a breath, making the fabric move across it. It also serves as a constant reminder to never let my guard down with Brody. This man that he's become will rip my heart out of my chest and make me watch as he savors each bloody bite.

Today is Christmas eve morning, and I haven't left this room. Every time I close my eyes, I see the blade sink into Papa's neck, and I can still feel the warmth of his blood running down my hand. I can't grieve because he doesn't deserve it, but I can't stay angry because I've become completely numb.

I try to conjure up Mama's face, her dark straight hair and vibrant brown eyes, but all I get is a blurry picture of how she looked. I miss her, and I'm hoping she's finally at rest. Now, as I look out the window, trying my darnedest to feel something, I think of Georgina and her mother, and how much I also want them to bleed. They are both vindictive and evil.

Brody has been keeping his distance, only coming

around to drop off food and then quickly leaving again. His now cold-shoulder attitude has left me questioning what his fucking motives are. What the fuck does he want with me?

I miss my guys; I want to be with them during this time since they are the only family I have left. I want Cooper's carefree attitude, Caine's domineering one, and Oliver's sense of comfort and stability. I miss being with them, and I just want to go home.

I hear the door open behind me, knowing it's Brody dropping off some sort of thrown together breakfast. Before I turn around, I wait to hear the tray drop and the door to close. I'm startled when I see him still standing there.

"Are you ready to continue now?" he asks, his arms crossed at his chest.

"Continue what?"

"The reason you're even here." He raises his brow.

"Oh, you mean I have a reason to be here other than to be raped and used for murder?"

He throws his head back as a hearty laugh escapes his mouth. I can't help but notice how beautiful his face is when he genuinely laughs. He looks boyish again, and that makes my heart ache.

"You want to know everything, right?" He wipes the fake tears from his eyes as he continues to chuckle. Always so fucking dramatic.

"Brody." I try to speak to his humanity. "What's the endgame? Where's Georgina?"

"I bet you want a chance at her and her mother, huh?" He's still wearing a shit-eating grin.

"Something like that." *Exactly like that.*

"Her mother will be easy to track down." He scratches at his chin. "Georgie, not so much."

"Why is that?" I ask him.

"Is that what you want to learn about today? Georgie's whereabouts?"

"Am I getting one thing a day?" I raise my brow.

"Yeah. I like to drag out the inevitable."

"What's the inevitable?" I cross my arms.

"Okay, did you want the inevitable today or Georgie?" His grin is so wide, like the fucking Cheshire Cat.

This asshole. "Georgie."

"Sit for this one." He points to the bed.

That doesn't sound suspicious at all. I walk to the bed and sit on it crossed-legged, waiting for him to start.

"Where to start." He taps his chin. "Okay, it really begins during freshman year, and my plan to take down my ex-best friend, Kailey. As you know, Georgina was never a fan of yours, and she volunteered herself along with the others to be your tormentors. The guys and I thought that was a good plan. That way none of the shit we thought up to do to you would ever come back on us, and it's normal for chicks to hate chicks." I roll my eyes and flip him the bird. He chuckles and leans forward to flick my nose, something he used to do whenever I did something he thought was cute. "The guys and I had more time to plan our futures this way, and the girls became obsessed."

"What were you planning?" I ask.

"Tsk." He wags his finger at me. "One a day."

"Right." I roll my eyes again.

"We have weekly meetings, the Golden Four. Well, we used to. They were usually held at the school library, but sometimes we'd have them here too. What I didn't know was Georgina had set up a listening device, and what pissed me off the most was that it was rudimentary at best. We missed it. We became complacent in our rules, and thought we were feared enough to never be fucked with. Georgina thought herself above it all too, and she thought she would never be suspected or caught. She admitted that she figured even if she were caught, I loved her enough to spare her."

"Did you love her?" I hate the way my stomach sours at the thought.

"That's what you want to know?" He smirks and leans forward, his breath fanning my face. "Out of everything I just told you, you want to know if I loved her?"

"Yes," I say, transfixed by his blue eyes.

"No." He sits back up. "I didn't love her. Anyway, things came to light the day you pulled Casey into the girl's bathroom at school. The things she told you would only ever come from one of the guys. They all swore up and down they didn't talk, and I believed them. They had just as much skin in the game as I did. It was Zeke that figured we were being listened in on. Thankfully, our more sensitive information was spoken about at school, and well, your stuff we spoke about here."

"Like my papa owing your family money."

"Yes." He nods. "The tape might've been played too, or we spoke about it, either or, we were being listened to. Zeke found the bug, and he traced it back to Georgie. When I questioned her, she denied it, and I let her believe she was encased in a safe little bubble. Zeke and I had a plan to interrogate her the night of Zeke's house party because I needed to know what else she knew, and what she'd already revealed to the others. Then you had my brother and Lance killed, and everything almost went to shit… Almost."

"I didn't have them killed." I shake my head. "Not that I will ever regret it happening."

"Whatever." He shrugs and continues, "In the aftermath's chaos that night, Zeke grabbed Georgie while I needed to get as far away from you as possible."

"Because you didn't believe me," I state.

"Well, yeah." He nods. "And I wanted to kill you. He brought her here to the very room I had your father in. That nasty one in the basement. He tied her up in the chair, then waited for me to come and start the proceedings."

My heart stops at that moment because I can already sense where this is going. Maybe anyone that finds themselves in that room winds up dead or crazy.

"It didn't take long for her to fess up to everything. She had heard the stuff about your father, and yes, she taunted you with certain things, but that was it. I pushed her a bit more and learned she did, in fact, tell her mother about your father's predicament, and I can only assume her mother then in turn, provided him with the solution."

"You mean having my mama killed for her insurance money? That solution?"

"The very same." So cold. "So, I deemed Georgina a traitor and disposed of her."

"Brody." My voice sounds a lot calmer than I'm feeling. "What do you mean, disposed of?" I watch with my breath held as he runs his thumb along his neck, croaking at the end. He fucking killed Georgina. "You killed her," I whisper, and his teeth shine bright with his wide grin.

"She wouldn't have lived a full life after that interrogation anyway," he adds nonchalantly.

My stomach turns, and I run to the bathroom just in time to empty its contents into the toilet. He tortured Georgina and killed her for listening in on him, for knowing information… Information he is giving to me freely. I heave again and groan when nothing comes up. He plans on killing me too, probably much in the same way, and I can't help but feel panicked and scared again.

"Almost done?" he calls out. "You really should eat."

I flush the toilet and rinse out my mouth. When I come back into the room, Brody is lying with his hands behind his head, his foot tapping out a silent beat.

"What are you going to tell people when they start to look for her?" I question him.

"That I haven't seen her since the night of Zeke's party. That's the truth, anyway. Georgina has been threatening her mother with running away for years. Once they see her bank account emptied and her passport missing, they'll begin a worldwide search, and that will take a long ass time."

"What did you do to her body?"

"That's all Zeke. I would assume it's similar to what happened to your papa's body." He grins at me.

"And what will happen to mine?" I try to hold in the tremors, but it doesn't work. I sound petrified, and I fucking am.

"I don't know what I'll do with your body, but I certainly know I'm not fucking done with it yet." He walks by me and once again flicks my nose. "By the way, Kailey, this house is rigged with surveillance. I fucking dare you to try and leave. I love a good chase."

I already know I'm not going anywhere. As much as I'm scared, I also want to know everything about these guys and what they are up to.

BRODY

TWENTY-TWO

I really wanted to rip that nasty pink nightgown off her body and claim her again, this time with her trying to fight her way out of it. I suppressed the urge, and instead, settled for telling her about Georgina.

Georgina would forever be the girl who became a traitor. I don't do well with traitors, as Charles can attest to, and Kailey is just lucky I decided not to view her as one. When I heard her accusation about Justin, I had a split second to react, and again, she's lucky I partially believed her.

Yes, from the first moment she muttered those words to me, I knew there was more than a possibility she was telling the truth, and I realized maybe she wasn't a traitor. But that doesn't mean she doesn't deserve the shit she got from us. I will never understand why we were dropped, why I was forgotten.

Justin and Lance were inseparable, like me and the three guys I call my brothers. I couldn't continue to deny the facts when they were blaring in my face. The accusations here at home, and the ones that followed them to Tulane. Maybe it's a good thing Caine and Cooper did what they did.

Tomorrow is Christmas, and it will be the first time I'm not alone on that day in many years. Justin rarely came home for the holidays, opting for exotic vacations instead. My parents can't stand to be in the same room, and the guys always had to spend that one day with their families. This year I will have the girl I once thought was my only family, and I can't wait until she sees what I got for her. It's taken years in the making.

My phone pings with a text, and I grin when I see the sender's name on my phone. Well, it looks like my day is about to get even more interesting. I head downstairs and out the front door, just in time to see his SUV pull to a stop. He slides out of the driver's seat and rounds the front.

"Well, well." I cross my arms over my chest. "Why would The Teacher be here to see me? Are you here to make a rescue call?"

"For whom exactly? Kailey or Charles?" Oliver grins. "You're lucky I'm the one who pays for the rehab facility he's in, and the one they called to say he had checked himself out. You and I both know that's bullshit." I don't bother to answer him, as he seems to think he has everything figured out. "We both know what Charles was expected to do, and you know what I do. So, given that I know your GPA score, I'm sure you can work out what this means."

"Get to the point, Teacher."

"I have now been given the task of taking you out because Charles hasn't checked in with my father in over a week. With that being said, you have a week until I am due to hunt you down. Take my fucking advice, Brody. Let Kail go and leave the country, start your life over."

"How would you explain that to your family?" I chuckle as he walks back to the driver's side.

"Let me worry about my family, and you worry about outsmarting the hunter."

I watch him get inside his SUV and burn his tires as he speeds away from my house. I have a few choices in front of me, but I think my first move would be to tell the guys exactly who The Teacher is.

"Bro, I barely got any sleep," Zeke curses into the phone.

"You can sleep when you're dead," I snarl. "This is important."

"Fine, I'll see you soon." He hangs up the phone, and I relax on my bed.

I'm not worried about being 'hunted' by The Teacher, but I am worried about what Kails will think about all this. I think it's time I tell her another bit of information, but this time Zeke will be listening too. He needs to be aware of everything in case something happens to me.

I'm guessing Zeke had to scrape his mother off the floor when he got home this morning if he still hasn't slept. His mother and mine could start up their own pharmacy if they wanted to. It must be what happens to females when they latch themselves onto a narcissistic man with power and money.

I get off the bed and make my way to Kailey's holding cell. She was sleeping not too long ago when I dropped off her dinner, so maybe she's awake now. I get to the door and listen. There's no sound inside. I slowly open the door to find the tray still full, and she's still lying on the bed. I would check her vitals if I couldn't see her chest moving with her deep breaths.

She left the curtains open so the light from the moon illuminated the skin on her legs, making them look like butterscotch on ice cream. I stand at the end of the bed and watch as she sleeps. The nightgown has twisted up around her thighs, and her hair is a wild mane around her head. Her face looks drawn, angry, and confused as she dreams about God knows what. Her lips move slightly, like she's mouthing the words in a book, and I stare at those lips.

Obsession, that's the only explanation for the way I'm feeling. It's always been an obsession when it came to Kailey-Himari, and no matter how much the hatred grew, the obsession grew as well. One was never without the other, and both of them never let me go. I had to see her, had to hate her, and I had to watch every fucking thing she did.

Obsession.

My track pants hit the floor, and my shirt is not too long after. I leave my boxers on because it's not about getting inside her right now. No matter how hard my cock is, I just want to curl around her and hope her warmth chases away my cold.

I crawl up the bed and wrap my arm around her waist, pulling her in tight against my body. She grows rigid and her breathing accelerates. She's awake.

"Brody," she croaks, half asleep.

"Don't ruin it with your fucking voice and stupid words," I growl quietly.

"Okay," she whispers, burrowing in tighter, then pressing her face against my neck.

My nose falls into her unruly hair, and I take a deep breath as her hand runs up my ribcage and around to my back.

Her nails bite into my skin as her fingers clench. I grab onto the fabric of her nightgown and drag it up slowly. It skims her thighs and slides up over her ass.

Her nails drag down my back, the sting making me feel something and awakening emotions I had long forgotten. My heart pounds, and I stop what I'm doing just to *feel* it. Her fingers meet the waistband of my boxers and slip inside. Her teeth nip at the skin on my neck, finally breaking me out of my enthrall.

I push her onto her back, nestling between her open thighs, and press my cock against her center. I can feel how wet she is through my boxers, and I can only wonder what she was dreaming about before I got in here, because surely, I didn't have this effect on her.

I push myself up and grab the thin fabric encasing her body, ripping it down the center. She gasps and arches her back, trying to bring herself closer to me.

Why, though?

It was only a few hours ago she learned I was a killer, and her stomach couldn't handle the words, let alone me. What happened?

"You are going to ruin all your mother's clothes," she whispers.

I press my weight back onto her and bring my mouth to her ear. "Why are you doing this?"

"It's what I've always wanted," she whispers back. "No matter how hard I try to despise you, hate you… I still fucking want you."

I push myself back up onto my hands and watch as she works my boxers down my legs. Can I do this? Can I be the man she's hoping for right now? Fuck her vanilla and then cuddle afterward?

"Why do you look like you're trying to solve an equation?" she asks with her brow raised.

I grab my cock in my hand and bring my body back on top of hers. Her hands find my back and her nails are once again embedding themselves into my skin.

"Shh… Stupid words," I whisper as I line myself up and slam inside of her.

She screams as I sink in about halfway and then continue to force myself in farther.

"Brody." Her head tosses, and she moans breathlessly.

Her pussy clenches around me, and I pull out, then slam back in. I haven't fucked like this before, me on top and facing the girl. If my dick is inside of a girl, I make it so I can't see her face. But watching Kailey's face right now is showing me how much I missed out on, or it's just because it's her face. I don't know.

Her hand comes up and caresses my cheek, reverently slow. Then the feel of her palm clapping against my face shocks me mid-thrust. Her eyes are filled with lust and anger as her hand once again meets my face.

"Continue to fuck me, asshole," she grits out, her hips pushing me the rest of the way inside of her. "At least fuck me like you mean it. Why are you making love to me?"

My cheek stings but my heart beats again, a fast staccato, and I can't hold back the snarl that comes out of my chest. I slip my hands under her thighs and angle her pelvis just right. I make sure my grip is tight, and when we're done here, my marks will remain on her thighs. I look down at her tits, seeing my initials burning red and angry against her skin. So fucking fitting. I lean over and run my tongue over the letters, her hiss the only sign it still hurts.

"You want to be fucked, right?" I ask as I pound into her.

She nods her head, putting on a brave face, but I see the way her throat constricts on her swallow. I scare her, and I can't help but grin at her fear.

"I'm sorry we don't have a pair of your panties here." I grab her throat forcefully. "My hand will have to do."

Her eyes widen at the realization that I've watched her with Oliver too, and she bucks under me. The monster inside of me wakes up along with my anger, and roars inside of my head as I pound inside Kailey.

I squeeze my fingers, feeling the sinewy tissue just beneath the skin of her throat. Just as I relax my grip, her hands smack at my chest and face. Anger red and hot courses through me, leaving a trail of heat under my skin. The hand not gripping her throat, grabs her thigh, lifting it higher on my waist, and I sink into a dark puddle of something that feels foul—depraved.

Suddenly, I'm locked inside of my body, helpless to stop anything, and privy to only watch what's happening in front of me. My hand stays clenched around Kailey's throat as she struggles to breathe, and her hands are trying to pry my fingers off of her. I'm still driving into her, my thrusts hard, and I try, but I can no longer feel her, or the way my heart was beating for her.

It's gone. Now… It's just him.

Her body shakes, and I try to take back control of my hand, but it's impossible. I'm here, slowly watching her die and hoping I will finish soon.

I'm cold here. My insides are vibrating as the chill seeps in, and my soul revels in the touch of this immoral dark pool I'm stuck in.

desecrated ESSENCE
ZEKE
desecrated ESSENCE

TWENTY-THREE

No one answers the door, and Brody isn't picking up his phone. I'm exhausted, and it's fucking bone deep. I'm tired of cleaning up everyone else's mess, my mother's and Brody's being the most tiring. I open the front door and sigh with relief when it's unlocked.

There's no noise in the house. It's hauntingly quiet, and once again, I'm not fucking sure what I'm walking into. I head up the stairs and straight to the room I know he's holding Kailey. It's late, so she's probably sleeping, but it's also Christmas Eve, and I want to see her.

I open the door to find Brody sprawled on top of Kailey. Both are naked, and both look passed out. I rush to the bed and pull Brody off of her. Her throat has his fingerprints in a deep shade of blue and more bruises dot her legs. The damage he's done to her is on full display right now, and I fucking feel myself lose it. I didn't entrust her to him so he could try to fucking kill her each day.

My fist connects with his mouth, and he begins to wake up. "Zeke?" I don't answer him as my fist flies out again, hitting him on the jaw, and he finally comes all the way to. "Kail!" he yells, and tries to get to her, but I pull him off the bed.

I punch him again in the stomach, and I watch with satisfaction as he crumbles to the floor.

"Zeke?" Her voice has me jumping on the bed and sitting her up. She sounds broken, in pain, and unsure of what the fuck happened.

"Bebelle." I run my fingers over her throat. "What happened?"

Her eyes widen and she frantically looks around the room, "Brody…"

"He's on the floor. I won't let him get to you."

"No, there's something wrong with him. He's not himself, Zeke." Her voice cracks on every other word, and the hoarseness of it makes me wince.

She pulls herself off the bed, then wraps the sheet around her body. I watch her rush to Brody's side and grab his face in her hands.

"Brody, look at me."

"I can't believe you would want anything to do with him after what he did." I know I sound disgusted, but fuck, I am.

"It wasn't him, Zeke. His eyes were blank, his body was like stone, and even his voice was off."

Fuck.

"He kept talking about himself in the third person. 'Brody is too soft with you.' He just kept repeating that, and then I passed out." Her fingers find her throat.

"He was choking you," I snarl. "Why? What was going on?" If she says he was raping her, I will kill him right now.

"Oh, god." She reaches under the sheet and her hand disappears between her legs. "We were… Oh, fuck." Her hands come out glistening with what only looks to be his cum.

"I can see what he was doing, but did you consent to this?" I'm shaking with anger, and it only grows every time her bruises come to light.

"Yes," she whispers, still staring at her fingers.

His groan has us both grabbing him and pulling him up to the bed. I got a few good hits in; his face is blooming with a few bruises.

"Fuck," he groans, and grabs onto his head.

"Brody." Her voice is a whisper, and he looks at her. "What happened?"

"Brody has a disorder…" I begin, but he stands abruptly and gets in my face.

"Stop!" he grits through his teeth, his spit flying.

"She's here to learn about us, right? That's what you told me, that she's here to learn everything, and finally accept us for who we are. She needs to learn about you too."

"What disorder?" she asks.

"Dissociative Identity Disorder," I say as Brody stalks out of the room. "Take the fucking meds!" I yell after him.

"Zeke, what is that?"

"He has a split personality that he's constantly fighting with. When his parents used him as a punching bag, he would dissociate and become a monster," I tell her as her face betrays her horror.

"The monster?" she whispers. "Oh, no."

"What? Did he call himself that when he hurt you?" I walk to her.

"When did this disorder start?" she asks, her eyes filling.

"He was diagnosed freshman year, but he said the monster has been with him since he was five or six. As he got older, it was harder to control it."

"Oh, god," she moans and sits on the bed. "This is all my fault."

"What? Bebelle, he has a disorder, it couldn't have come from you."

"But it did." She nods as her shoulders shake. "When we were young, Brody would tell me about when his father would hit him, or his mother would yell at him, and I told him he had to be brave. I told him he had to become like them, so that when he was older and bigger, he could fight them back. Zeke," a sob catches in her throat, "I told him to become the monster."

When he was older and bigger, he could fight them back. I feel the goose bumps flare across my skin and my mouth dries with a realization. Could Kailey planted the idea in Brody's head, and it became what it is today?

"I ruined him, and then I dropped him. Oh god, Zeke, you were right, this is all my fault," she cries, and I stand still, letting everything absorb.

Brody walks back in with his hand clasped in front of him and a bottle of water. He opens his fist and sitting in his palm are three different pills.

"Happy?" he asks as he pops them in his mouth, then guzzles the water. "I don't like how they make me foggy and slow thinking." He faces Kailey. "I didn't want to hurt you that time, he just—"

"The monster, Brody," she cuts him off. "That's who *he* is, right?"

Brody's face becomes still, and I recognize this as his business face, the one that reveals nothing.

"Zeke told me," she mumbles.

Brody looks at me with his jaw clenched and his hands in fists, the knuckles white.

"She deserved to know what happened. You could have killed her. Look at her neck," I implore.

His head turns slowly and surveys her sitting there wrapped in a sheet, battered and bruised.

"You look sexy as all hell with my handprints on you." He grins at her, and shockingly, she has a hint of a smirk on her face too.

"Fuck's sake, what is this?" I look between them. "What was I called here for?"

Kailey gets up and makes her way into the bathroom as Brody sits on the bed she vacated.

"I need to tell you both something I found out," he says as his hand swipes through his hair.

"Are you feeling alright?" I ask him.

"Yeah, I have to say it fast before these pills numb my brain."

"She told me where the monster came from," I tell him as I lean against the wall. "Y'all created him when y'all were kids."

"We didn't create him; he's always been there. We just gave him a name that day," he mumbles.

Kailey comes out of the bathroom and hurries into Brody's mother's closet. He's watching her closely, and I can see his demeanor has changed from earlier. She steps back out in a bright pink, velour tracksuit, and I snort.

"Think that's funny?" She turns, and I full out laugh when I read 'Juicy' on her ass.

She sits next to Brody, and he reaches over to tuck a lock of hair behind her ear. Almost sweet, until I see the marks on her throat.

"What did you want to tell us?" I ask.

"Kails." He turns to look at her. "What I am about to tell you next is the complete truth, and if you want to call him after, you can do so."

"Okay," she whispers.

"The Ballons have a deadly assassin on their payroll. He has to accept one hit per year and agree to train others when they ask him."

"Fuck," I groan under my breath. I know where this is going.

"No." Kailey shakes her head vehemently. Apparently, so does she. "No, Brody. I won't believe it."

"Let me finish, and then you can call him," Brody says calmly.

When neither of us disagrees, he continues.

"That's how he got his name, The Teacher. He trains other assassins, although his father has yet to find one like him. He has the expertise to kill every target and dispose of them too. He's never missed a target."

"The Teacher." Kailey looks at him. "That's why you call

him that."

"Yeah. We know Charles was working with the Ballons to kill me, and now that they haven't been able to get a hold of him, they asked The Teacher to do the job."

"Oliver would never kill you." Kailey is still shaking her head.

"He'd have no choice," I cut in. "He said he would be away for a few days. Said it was family shit."

"I have a week to get my shit together." Brody nods and looks from me to Kailey. "He came by earlier to let me know the deadline."

"I want to call him," she demands while holding out her hand.

I hand her my phone and watch as she dials his number. The phone rings and rings until his voicemail comes up.

"Oliver, call me back at this number. It's an emergency." Kailey's voice is wavering as she tries to hold in her panic.

Then we sit in silence, waiting for the phone to ring anxiously. I want Brody to be wrong to save Kailey from any more heartbreak, but I knew there was something up with Oliver, and this all fits.

"I have to tell the others."

"Yeah." Brody nods.

"No!" Kailey yells, her voice still hoarse. "Do not turn the others on him. What if it's not real?"

"It's real," Brody tells her. "Have I fucking lied to you yet?"

"If it is true," she gets up and paces, "he has no choice."

"No, he doesn't," Brody agrees. "I don't hold anything against him for that in particular, but there are other things that make me want to kill him slowly."

"Who don't you want to kill, Brody?" she snaps at him, and I laugh at the surprised look on his face.

"She's right, though," I continue to chuckle.

"And what about you?" She turns on me. "You secured my house from any intruders, and this fucker was still getting in. You fucking knew he was getting in, didn't you?"

"Not at first." I hold my hands up. "But I just want to say, I fucking hate apples."

"Oh, my god!" She stomps her foot, and it's the most adorable thing I've seen.

"Zeke is our tech man. He has his own security firm and has been working on all security details for us," Brody says. "You need to know that when we need someone looked into for anything, he's our man. He kept a steady watch on your father."

"And you get rid of bodies?" She looks at me.

"Only two so far." I hold up my hands. "That's usually Cooper's job."

"Cooper?!" She swings around and pins Brody with a glare.

"Another day," he states and gets up. "My head is getting foggy, and I need to get some rest."

"Do these drugs work?" Kailey asks him, concern clear in her eyes.

"They suppress my subconscious thoughts. I feel like I can't concentrate on anything too long, and that way he's suppressed too."

"Monster," she whispers.

KAILEY HIMARI

TWENTY-FOUR

Before Zeke left, I tried calling Oliver another three times, and left him a slew of text messages. He's clearly avoiding me and that means everything is true. He's an assassin known as The Teacher, and his next hit is Brody.

I don't know how to feel about any of this, and with everything that's happened the last few days, my mind is reeling. I'm still trying to conjure up some semblance of feeling other than anger, but it's not working. I'm angry at all of them for hiding so much from me, at Brody for punishing me, at my papa for ruining our family, and mostly at myself for living in a secluded bubble for so long.

There are things I can never forgive myself for, and I just added shutting out my best friends as one of them. I need to face the consequences of my actions, and not just the effect it had on my life, but also on theirs.

It's Christmas morning, and my body is sore. Walking

is difficult, and swallowing is painful. I'm not a stranger to spending Christmas alone. Last Christmas, Papa had to work—apparently—and the Christmas before that was the same. I lost that nostalgic feeling for holidays when Mama was killed. Something else Papa deprived me of.

Then, the revelation about Brody and Monster has been constantly on my mind. I can't completely forgive him for what he's done to me, especially since he's held me here, but I can't completely disregard his mental health. As much as I want to hate him, and even though I've told him as much… I can't.

While he was inside of me yesterday, after I slapped him, I watched his whole demeanor change. His face changed, his eyes changed, and his voice changed. I thought he was possessed, and as I felt myself losing consciousness, I accepted that death was there to take me.

He had become Monster.

I hear the door open, and Brody steps in to drop a plate of what looks like waffles again. "Merry Christmas." His voice sounds better, has some pitch to it. He throws a box wrapped in a bow on the bed.

"You got me something?" I ask as I walk toward the bed.

"Nah, that has taken years to make." He leans against the wall and puts his hands in his pockets. "I took the meds again, so if you want to talk about something, we have to do it now."

"Can you tell me about this empire you and the guys are making?" I ask as I pick up the box. It's light, and when I shake it, there's no noise inside.

"We hate our families." He shrugs. "We wanted to watch them fall from their pedestals as we climbed ours."

"How so?"

"Zeke, for instance, was supposed to take over his father's import/export business. Any guesses as to what he's importing or exporting?"

"Drugs?" I suggest.

"That's one."

"Weapons?"

"You're good at this." He grins, the slight curve making his face devastating.

"Is there more?"

"His most lucrative asset would be humans," he states, and I let the words sink in.

"Like slaves?"

"Skin trade, yeah." He nods. "Mostly children."

"Oh, my god." My hand covers my mouth. "Zeke is taking that over?"

"Zeke has effectively put his father out of business. He tracks all his shipments, then frees them before their intended destinations. Now, his father owes a lot of powerful people money or products, and he can't deliver either. He's on the run currently, and Zeke is trying to locate him for those very people."

"Zeke is setting his father up to die?"

"Precisely." He scratches at his chin.

"And Cooper cleans up dead bodies?"

"Cooper's family business is to clean up or cover up murders and provide security detail to high-profile clients. Cooper instead started his own clean up business, stealing many clients from his father. He also pairs up with Zeke in security detail." He grins again, obviously proud of his closest friends.

"His father is just about through too."

"You and Caine?"

"Let's try again tomorrow." He nods at the box. "Are you going to open that?"

"I'm scared," I whisper.

"Good."

I finger the silky-smooth texture of the bright red ribbon and its contrast against the dark navy box. I pull on the bow, and the ribbon comes apart smoothly. I gather it up and slip it into the pocket of my pants. If whatever is in this box is meant to torture me, at least something beautiful was attached. I open the lid and stare inside at the contents.

"One for each day since you left me." His voice is closer than before, and I look up to find him leaning on the bed. "One for each day I was without your mother's warmth."

Inside the box, there are hundreds of purple Wisteria petals. Some completely dried out and crumbled, others in the process of drying, but there's a few on top that are still a vibrant purple color. This means Brody has been at my house every day for the past four years.

"Why are you giving me this?" I end on a sob.

"You needed to be reminded about that tree, about that gazebo, and what you both meant to me at one time."

The gazebo that stands covered by chaotic, beautiful vines, completely closed off to the outside world, and forgotten about.

"Let those be your reminder. Everything that lives will one day dry up and crumble into the earth. So live each day like you are vibrant and free, because before you know it, your essence is blowing in the wind."

He doesn't say anything else as he flicks my nose and gets up, walking out of the room. I look back into the box and look at the petals, vibrant and free, just like Mama was. I pick up the newest petal and press it to my nose. Its fragrance reminds me of sitting inside the gazebo and reading a book with Mama, the scent conjuring her face the clearest I have seen it since she has passed. I can hear the soft tinkle of her laugh and see the way she would toss her head.

This entire box is the best gift anyone has ever given me.

ZEKE

TWENTY-FIVE

"Oliver is Ballons' assassin, The Teacher?" Cooper looks as white as a sheet. "How the fuck did we miss this?"

"We became indolent and completely consumed with Kailey," Caine answers.

"That's not a bad thing," I tell him.

"Of course it's not." He shakes his head. "It's the truth, nonetheless. We are more than capable of accomplishing both."

"We can't let him kill Brody." Cooper stands and paces.

They've been staying at Kailey's house since she left, needing to be close to her in some capacity, and I decided I would stay here too. I have to completely cut my mother off, and since my father is on the run, there's no other family for me anyway.

"We can't take on the Ballons." Caine scratches his cheek. "It would be impossible, and we're not ready to make our business known yet. We need to become more established and stable. This would show Kennedy we're his competition and he could easily take us out."

He's right, as per usual, Caine is our logical thinker, and when he and Brody mastermind together, it's explosive.

"How is your new boy from Canada doing? Danny, right? Can we send him after Oliver?" Cooper is grasping at straws.

"He's good, but not that good. Come on, The Teacher has been killing since he was thirteen years old, and never losing a target." Caine looks at him like he's lost his mind.

"What are our options?" I ask Caine.

"We're going to have to stake out Brody's place."

"Yes!" Cooper exclaims. "We can see Kailey."

Yeah... That can't happen. If they see the state she's in with the bruising, Caine and Cooper will kill Brody for Oliver.

"I'll talk to Brody tonight and see what he wants to do. He's pissed we took Kailey from him," I tell them.

"He was all for it at the beginning of the school year." Cooper shakes his head.

"Because he didn't think it would work, Coop." Caine, always on point. "I think he always thought it would be him and her one day."

He's probably right, Brody would have thought that way before, but now? I don't think he wants her, but he also doesn't want anyone else to have her.

"I'll talk to him," I placate them.

"I don't care if he doesn't let us in. We will stake out his house from all other angles," Caine growls, and I know he means what he says.

"Then what?" I look at them both. "We kill Oliver?"

"Would you rather he kills Brody?" Caine asks.

He's right. If it comes down to it, we will have to kill Oliver to save Brody. He's our brother before anything else. We made a pact a long time ago and nothing can destroy that. Except Kailey, all of them being in love with her could cause a fucking war.

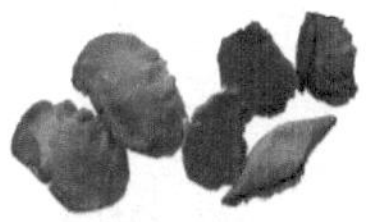

The house again looks desolate and vacant. With how big this property is and the size of the house, we are going to have a problem with protection. We will have to bring in a few of our mercenaries, or Caine's assassins. We would still run the risk of being sniped off, one by one.

The Teacher, we learned, is a trained sniper and also specializes in bombs. So pretty much we're fucked. He's an expert at making the deaths look like an accident or the targets just disappearing, never to be heard from again. To say we're nervous is a fucking understatement.

I'm walking through the unlocked front door again, and growl in frustration. *Make it easy for him, why don't you, jackass?* I head up the stairs with a few bags in tow and stop at the top. To the right is Brody, and to the left is Kailey, unless Brody has smothered Kailey with his body again, or better yet, broke her fucking neck.

Left it is.

I rush to her door, having already convinced myself she's dead, and frantically enter the room. Dropping the bags by the door, I rush to the bed.

"Zeke?" She's sitting on the bed with tears on her cheeks, and an open box sitting between her legs.

"What happened?" I ask her as I quickly scan her for fresh injuries.

"Nothing." She quickly closes the box and brushes away her tears. "What are you doing here?"

"Are there body parts in there? Dead mice?"

"No." She shakes her head and smiles at me. "Just a weird gift."

"Oh, okay. I came to see Brody about this whole Oliver situation."

"You told the others?" she asks me.

"Yeah, you know I had to."

"I know," she sniffs. "They're going to kill him, aren't they?"

"Not if he doesn't kill Brody."

"He hasn't tried to call me back." She looks at me with those large hazel eyes. "Why doesn't he want to talk to me?"

"Probably because you're the only one that could talk him out of that obligation."

"I have no other choice; I have to lose one of them." She shakes her head.

"Last time I was here, I thought the choice would be clear, and now it looks like you don't want to lose Brody either."

"What can I say?" His voice filters into the room. "I grow on people."

"That's not true at all." I turn to him with a snort.

He looks a lot better today. His eyes look clearer, and his voice is back to its normal pitch.

"I see you scrutinizing me. I took the meds." He grins as he comes into the room.

"I can tell." I nod.

"Tell me. When do the others plan on storming the place?" He and Caine always thought alike.

"I told them you wouldn't want them inside, so they promised to watch from outside."

"I figured." He taps his fingers on his arm. When he's on his meds, his worry manifests differently. He taps his fingers when he's nervous. Without the meds, he'd be doing something violent. "You can't let them do that. They're a weak point for me, and Oliver will use that to his advantage."

"Okay, I can tell them that. I'll also need to give them a plan, bro. If I don't, they'll gladly come here and die for you."

"Give me two days," he implores. "I got some shit to finish up." He's looking at Kailey, and I feel he's gearing up to say goodbye.

"The bruising is looking a little better." I point at her throat. The purple and dark blue are lightening up.

"Brody has been giving me ice for it." She smiles at me.

"The guys sent me over with a few gifts." I point at the bags. "There's something from each of us."

"I wasn't able to get you guys anything." She glares at Brody, and he shrugs.

"They already have enough trinkets from girls over the years." He chuckles, and I punch his arm.

"I'll get you guys something as soon as I can." She smiles

at me.

I grab the bags by the door and bring them over to the bed. I reach inside the first one and bring out a horribly wrapped gift from Cooper.

"I don't know what to say." She laughs when I hand it to her.

"Cooper?" She holds what's obviously something made from fabric.

"What gave it away?" I roll my eyes.

She giggles as she rips open the paper and holds up a purple cashmere sweater. It's the same color as the Wisteria tree in her backyard, and she gasps as she holds it to her chest.

"Interesting," Brody mumbles as he continues to tap his fingers

"So soft." Her voice is muffled from her face being buried into the sweater.

"Next." I pull out a red gift bag with green tissue sticking out of the top.

"Caine?" she asks.

"Um, no." I shake my head. "That was found in your room, presumably left by Oliver."

"Oh!" She rips the paper off the top and looks into the bag. Her head pops back up quickly, and a bright red stains her cheeks.

"The suspense is killing me," Brody drawls, and I snicker.

"I can't." She shakes her head.

Brody leans forward and snatches the bag, peeking inside.

"Wow," he whistles. "Red, huh?"

He pulls out a red corset and thong set, something Kailey would look amazing in. Now I'm hard, in track pants, with nothing to hide it.

"I wore something like that to Georgina's party."

"And he obviously saw you in it," Brody teases, then throws the bag back on the bed.

"Next," I clear my throat as I try to think of anything else to deflate my pulsing dick.

I hand her a meticulously wrapped gift with a matching bow and ribbon.

"Caine." She grins widely as she opens it.

Inside is a very expensive bottle of red wine. I don't see any connection, and it's actually a very impersonal gift. She gasps and holds it to her cheek.

"I have ten others like it in the cellar. Relax." Brody rolls his eyes.

"Of course, you wouldn't know what this is," she snaps at him.

"Should I?"

"It was the bottle used at Caine's house for Spin the Bottle." When neither of us responds, she growls in frustration. "The first night Caine and I kissed."

"Huh," Brody grunts.

I can't believe either of them remembered the fucking bottle we spun that night.

"Here's mine." I hand her the small rectangular gift. "It's nowhere near as special as these other ones."

"I'll determine that, thank you," she huffs as she takes

the gift. She rips it open and squeals with excitement. "No way!" She jumps up on the bed, waving the object in the air.

"Is that a controller?" Brody asks as he tries to get a good look at what's in her hand.

"It's the Nintendo Switch controller!" She jumps on the bed.

"The console is hooked up at your house waiting for you when you get home," I tell her.

"This is the best Christmas ever!" she squeals one more time and falls back onto the bed.

That says a lot, considering she killed her father and is being held here against her will.

BRODY

TWENTY-SIX

My brothers are clearly in love with Kailey, including Zeke. I guess you can throw The Teacher into the mix, as well. I can see the time and care they put into her gifts to make it personal. I had never planned to let her go, in fact, I wanted to kill her when I was through, but for some reason, I want to see her home and playing with that fucking game console she was so excited about.

To hear her say this was her best Christmas made me want to resurrect her father and kill him myself. We had Christmas with her mother, but Sara wasn't much for the holiday because she wasn't raised with it. Charlie had been dropping the ball with his daughter for many years.

I open my current journal and review all the notes I have gathered on Kailey. Since having her in my house, I have filled nearly a whole booklet on timelines and theories. Mind you, this shit is hard to read, given I wrote some of them in explosive rages.

One particular timeline has been bothering me since I first heard it. Georgina manipulated my brother and Kailey, ultimately ending up with him violating her. All the clues add up, and I can't ignore that my brother certainly had something to do with Kailey's extreme change before high school. So did Georgina. She paid for her deceit, yes, but I could've made it so much worse if only I knew the full extent. As for Justin, it's hard to pull apart the love I feel for him as my brother from the betrayal I feel for what he did to Kailey.

He of all people knew what she meant to me, and he knew what the fucking consequences would be for defiling her. She was so young, and it makes my insides quake whenever I think about what she went through, at both of their hands.

After all this time, I'm finally understanding what Cooper and Caine did, and I am trying to let go of the love I have for Justin. It's hard because love doesn't come easy for me, and I have only ever loved two people. After today, I will love no one.

I run my fingers over the deep pencil indents on the page and read through the scratches. Georgina found out about Charles and her mother. This put her in a rage since she always was jealous of Kailey, and she planned to ruin my best friend for the rest of her life. Maybe she had hoped Kailey would spill the beans, and then her father would have to end things with her mother to soothe his daughter at home. What she didn't expect was Charles hiring my brother to kill his wife that very same night, freeing him up to be with Cassy for good.

I hurry to write what will most probably be my last entry, and slam the journal shut. These fucking meds make me tired, and thinking logically is a strenuous activity. At least it keeps him quiet for the time being. I know I will have to stop taking them to stand a chance against The Teacher, but for now, they keep me calm, and I can at least sleep.

The feeling of the bed moving and the blankets rustling has me jolting awake to grab the intruder by their very soft—very purple—sweater.

"What the fuck?" I focus on my fisted hand in the material of said purple sweater.

"Brody, it's me Kailey." I close my eyes at the sound of her voice and try to calm down. "Sorry, I just couldn't sleep."

"It's fine." I release the sweater slowly and lie back down. "I would suggest waking me before sneaking into my bed, Kails."

"Yeah, probably smart," she says as she lies down beside me. "I hate this bed."

"What the fuck did it ever do to you?" I turn my face to look at her.

"It's where you did awful things to me," she whispers.

"Me, Kails. I did awful things, not the fucking bed. You sound like an idiot," I growl.

I'm shocked when I hear her giggle. "You admit you did awful things to me?"

"Did you get into my mother's stash again? Of course, I admit it. I planned it and much worse. You fucking got off easy."

"I actually only got off once," she snorts.

"Are you making a joke out of the torture I spent so much time planning for?" I look at her incredulously.

"What else can I do about it, Brody?" She looks at me with a grin ghosting her perfectly plush lips.

"I don't know." I shrug. "Kill me in my sleep?"

"Can we just burn this bed instead?"

"That's your problem. You lay blame on things that actually have nothing to do with what's happened to you," I snarl.

"Like I did with you four."

"Something like that, yeah." I shake my head.

"I'm sorry, Brody. I am so sorry I hurt you," she cries.

"You cry a lot." I stare at her tears. "It's so fucking exhausting to watch, and I can only imagine it's exhausting to physically do it."

"Are you listening?" She raises her voice, its sound an annoying pitch. "I'm sorry!"

"How can I ignore you?"

She gets up and straddles my waist, her hands landing on my stomach. She's wearing the fucking sweater and nothing else. What the fuck was she thinking, coming in here like that? Her hands are freezing, and the cold is seeping through my bare skin.

"I won't let Oliver kill you. I'm not leaving you here, and you need to accept my apology." Her fingertips dig into my flesh.

"How so? Why not? And who says?"

"Brody!" she growls, grabbing my chin in her hand.

I slap her wrist, and her hand flies to the side. "Don't be deceived by the calm exterior I am exuding. I will still hurt you if you dare try to lay your hands on me."

"Maybe that's what I want." Her hand comes back to my chin. She's fucking daft.

"Your black and blue neck states otherwise." I slap her hand away again, this time harder.

"How much more punishment do I need to take before you forgive me?"

"Kails," I flip us around, and lay her on her back, "I wanted your punishment to end in death. There was no forgiveness."

"You really are going to kill me." Her eyes widen, and those never-ending fountains start up again.

I'm annoyed by her constant stream of tears and her whiney fucking voice, but my cock is all too happy to be pressed up against her. Her wide eyes darken when she feels the evidence of my arousal pressing into her.

I growl and lift myself off of her. This is not what I intended to do, and I would rather not be surrounded by a cloud of lust for the remaining time she's here.

"Don't." Her hands grab my biceps and try to lock me in place. "Don't deny this."

I lower my face to hers, letting our noses touch, and I speak slowly. "You want me to fuck you again, Kails?"

"Yes." Her answer is sure and confident. "But I want to be conscious of it all this time. Do you think you can accomplish that?"

My body moves of its own accord, and I crush my boxer-clad cock into her wet, bare pussy. "What makes you think I even want to?"

"Your hard dick." She raises a brow.

"Oh, come on," I sneer. "Your pussy was wet when I was forcing you too."

"Fine." Her face reddens with anger. "Get off of me."

She pushes at my chest, and my cock jerks against her.

"Oh, you want me to fight you? Is that the only way you like it?" Her face becomes cruel, and I lean forward to lick her cheek.

"I am like my brother, right?"

"Are you proving to me you're cruel and demeaning? I already know that, Brody. So either fuck me or get off." She raises her brow, and I blow all caution to the wind.

"Fine." I pull down my boxers and line myself up to her soaking wet pussy. "Since you keep begging for it." Then I inch inside of her.

"Beg for it?" she shrills and bucks underneath me, only aiding me to slide in farther.

"This pussy is tight for being around the block, Kails," I groan as I thrust the rest of the way in.

"I should've forced you to wear a condom, Brody. You used to fuck Georgina," she snaps in my face.

I pull out while leaning up so I can watch myself disappear back inside of her again. She sucks me in, her juices saturating my balls, and her moan cuts off any other snide comments she has in mind.

So this is what normal sex is like? Kind of mundane and simple, and it's shocking, but I like it.

"Harder, Brody," she moans, and I grin. Sure thing.

I grab her thighs and lift her legs up and onto my shoulders. Her pussy opens up, then I begin a punishing rhythm that has her screaming her pleasure.

"Oh god," she pants. "Don't stop."

Her pussy grows tighter, and I know she's about to come

all around my dick. I've wanted this moment since my dick started growing hard for her around twelve years old. I slam into her and grind myself against her clit, making her gasp. Her nails sink into my biceps, and I watch her face closely as she comes undone.

She screams my name, and her body trembles with the force of her orgasm.

"Kiss me," she pants, and I stop moving, dropping her legs from my shoulders. "Please."

I bring my lips a breadth's width from hers. "No."

Then I continue to pump inside of her, chasing my orgasm and ignoring the glare she's firing at me. She can be pissed all she wants. I let her come, didn't I?

My orgasm rushes in at me, and I only have a split second to decide whether or not I want to come in her. Fuck it, I'll let her have the pleasure of my seed coating her insides, and this time, I can be the one to feel what it's like to come raw inside a girl. It's not something I have ever done before.

Her eyes roll back as she once again clenches around me, milking my cock for every single drop and holding me in her tight grip.

I pull out and roll over onto my back on the bed, trying to bring my breathing back under control. Boring, vanilla sex may not be so boring after all.

"Fuck, I really can't stand you," she huffs and gets off the bed. "You are such an arrogant asshole."

She's standing there with just the sweater on, and her hands clenched at her sides. I watch as the evidence of our vanilla sex runs down her thigh.

"Kails," I say as I fold my hands behind my head.

“What?”

“You got a little something there on your thigh,” I point out and watch as she looks down.

“Argh!” She stomps her foot and storms out of the room, yelling, “I hate you!” Over her shoulder.

KAILEY HIMARI

TWENTY-SEVEN

He is an insufferable asshole! I don't know why I thought I could bring out the Brody I once knew. He's too far gone, and his distrust for me is something hard-wired in his brain. He loves to hurt me and watching me suffer because it is a bonus.

I turn on the shower and step inside. I need to wash his scent off of me. I can't believe I let him fuck me without a condom, and then do nothing to stop him from coming in me. This isn't me, and I know exactly what's happening. I am looking for his forgiveness, no matter the cost.

I can't do it anymore; I can't put myself through this any longer, and staying here is not helping. I can't leave until I come face-to-face with Oliver though, because when I make a promise, I fucking keep it. I won't let Oliver kill Brody.

I fucked him in Cooper's gift. I stick my face into the spray and try to rinse the shame off of me. I went in there hoping to end it with his cock hard and driving into me. My hand skates across my stomach and down over my folds. I wanted to taste him so badly. I wanted his kiss, and he made a fool out of me by refusing. My fingers tease open my pussy as I think about our previous kisses, all-consuming and bruising.

I dip in one finger and then another, as I fuck myself to visions of Brody. In my visions, he wants me more than just to fuck. He makes love to me and kisses me like I'm the most precious thing in his life.

Shame, thick and heavy, coats me when I should be thinking of the four guys who actually feel these things for me. Instead, I'm here pining for the one who couldn't care if he tried.

The shower door opens just as I moan mid-stroke, and I turn my head in shock.

"Heard the shower and thought I'd wash myself off too." His eyes fall to my hand nestled deep between my legs and his smile is wide.

"What?" I ask, trying to save myself further embarrassment. "Am I not allowed to finish myself off?"

His head tosses back with a laugh, "I finished you off twice, Kails."

"Sure, but it feels so much better when I envision one of the others instead."

His facial expression doesn't change. If anything, he is unaffected by what I just said, and why would he care? I'm just a pussy for him to fuck or rape.

I move aside as he submerges himself under the spray. His body is perfection, wrapped in a golden exterior, and the worst part is he knows it. He fucking knows his appeal, and yet he doesn't give a shit about what people think or how he should appropriately act.

"You're staring at me, Kails." He turns and flicks my

nose.

"I'm trying to figure out why you couldn't shower in your own room."

"They are all my rooms." He shrugs. Asshole.

I continue to stare at him, hoping to make him uncomfortable enough that he'll just leave, and I can shower in peace.

"Whose gift was your favorite?" he asks.

"I don't know." I shrug. I do know.

"Well, you fucked me in Cooper's gift. Maybe not that one." He chuckles.

"I was horny thinking of him while I wore the sweater, and you were all that was available," I snap.

"I'd believe that if you weren't begging me to kiss you during the whole thing," he continues to laugh. "Caine's was thoughtful, but kind of simple. Zeke got you something he knew you would enjoy. Was it his?" I don't answer as I reach around him and grab the shampoo. "Or maybe The Teacher's? Did it bring back memories of fucking him in something similar?"

What the fuck?

"Tell me you weren't watching that too?"

"Nope, but I'm suddenly wishing I had." He grins as the water cascades down his chest and bows over his hard cock. I look back up at him with a raised brow. "What?" He gazes down at himself. "I can't help it. My initials on your tit are distracting."

I look down at the healing and scabby letters. It is distracting against my otherwise unblemished skin.

"You want me to say your gift was my favorite?" I ask him.

"What? No." He shakes his head. "I gave you a bunch of dead and dying petals."

"You gave me Mama," I whisper.

"What?" He's looking at me like I've grown an extra head.

"It's the first time I've seen her face clearly for a long while." I step under the spray to wash the shampoo out of my hair.

When I open my eyes again, he's so close I can see each individual bristle of hair on his face.

"I can't give you what the others do, you understand that, right? I'm not your boyfriend, and nor will I ever be. I don't want to make love to you because I don't love you, I don't want to kiss you because inside, you'll flare with hope for something that will never happen, and I can't keep you in this house because I see you softening to me."

His words stab into my heart and slice it open to bleed everywhere. I don't know how he can just say all that and act like those words aren't weapons created to decimate me.

"Are you letting me go?" My voice croaks as I struggle to hold in my tears.

"Are you going to cry again?" He huffs and opens the shower door. "You must be dehydrated by now." And then he slams it shut in my face.

Maybe it's best I leave and help the guys to keep Brody alive, because if I stay here, I'm the one who's going to die a slow and agonizing death.

BRODY

She's sleeping with tears drying on her face and her mouth turned down into a frown. I can't let Kailey fall in love with a monster, even though I hate her. I don't want to see her destroyed any longer, and I know if she continues to stay here, the damage will be irreversible.

I meant the words I said in the shower, and when I saw her heart break in front of me, I knew it was time to end this. Does she deserve a happy life with children and that white picket shit everyone is always looking forward to? No. I want her to have a chaotic life filled with as much misery as there is happiness. Highs that make her feel invincible and lows that have her wishing she was dead, and most of all, I want her to experience every single facet of color in the brightest and darkest tints that ever existed.

I brush her hair out of her face, and she sucks in a breath, saying my name on the exhale. My heart feels like it's squeezing inside my chest, only solidifying my decision to send her home.

I pull out my phone and dial the number I'm looking for.

"Asshole." Caine's voice comes through the speaker.

"Come and get her out of my house." I hang up and lean over her angelic sleeping face.

"I hate you a little less," I whisper, and press my lips to hers softly.

I get up and grab my bag off the floor, pulling it up and over my shoulder. I will make a promise to her right here and right now. If I make it out of this alive, I will make sure she has the life I know she deserves.

ZEKE

TWENTY-EIGHT

"He really called and said to come get her?" My heart is pounding, and my palms are sweating.

When the guys see the state of Kailey's body, Brody will be dead. No need for Oliver and his theatrics.

"Yeah." Caine jumps into his truck. "You can ride with me."

Thankfully, Caine and I are going there alone since Cooper is home with his family, and Oliver is out stalking Brody. I don't really want to drive him, because once he realizes I saw her that way and let her stay, I'm dead, too.

Fuck it. Time to face the music of the decisions I made and hope they see my reasoning. I hop up into the passenger side and hang on while Caine rips out of the driveway onto the road.

The drive to Brody's is quick, way too quick to plan and avoid certain death.

"Place looks fucking deserted," Caine mutters as he gets out of the truck.

"It's always like this."

"I'm glad to be taking her home. I need to sleep, and I can't seem to do it while she's here," he growls, and he prowls up to the front door.

"It's probably open," I tell him as I come up behind.

He opens the door and looks back at me with confusion. "He's taking his meds, right?"

"Yeah." I nod. "He did the last time I was here."

"He's a fucking lunatic."

Yeah, you don't know the half of it.

"She's in his parents' bedroom," I tell him, watching as he storms up the stairs.

As he rushes into that room, I hook a left at the stairs, and head to Brody's room. I open the door and step in. First thing I notice is there's no Brody, and next is a piece of paper folded on the bed. I walk to it and pick it up. I open it and see his chicken scratch writing.

BROTHERS,
I WANTED TO WATCH HER SUFFER
MORE THAN OUR HIGH SCHOOL
ANTICS COULD PROVIDE. SOMETHING
INSIDE OF ME NEEDED REVENGE
LIKE MY NEXT BREATH, BUT IN
TRYING TO BREAKING HER, I'M
AFRAID I BROKE MYSELF INSTEAD.

THE TEACHER IS BREATHING DOWN
MY BACK, AND ALL I CAN THINK
ABOUT IS MAKING SURE SHE'S NOT
IN THE CROSSFIRE.

I'LL BE AROUND IF I SURVIVE,
B.L.

Fuck. I stand from the bed to see Caine standing in the doorway, his body rigid with anger.

"Did you see her while you were here?" His words are clipped and filled with seething.

"Yeah." I nod.

"Caine!" I hear Kailey yell from the hallway. "Do not blame him!"

She rushes into the room and stands between us.

"Kailey, it's okay. Go grab your stuff," I tell her.

"No." She shakes her head. "Caine, I chose to stay here even though Brody wasn't himself. Zeke tried to get me to come home."

She's lying to someone she loves for me.

"No, she didn't." I ease her aside. "I trusted Brody when he said he had a plan, and I failed her."

"Stop!" she screams as Caine advances on me, his hands fisted.

"We'll sort this out later," he snarls, and I know he means when Kailey isn't around.

"Yeah." I nod.

He snatches the paper out of my hand and rips it open to read it.

"Zeke, come with me." Kailey grabs my hand, leading me back to the other bedroom. "Where's Brody?"

"He didn't say anything to you about leaving?" I ask her.

"No." She shakes her head. "We fought, and then I fell asleep."

"My guess is he's getting a head start on Oliver."

"I need to get a hold of Oliver." Her eyes bore into mine.

"I don't know him well enough to help with that." I shrug.

"Zeke, I remember what Brody said. You can track down anyone."

"I can't track him down, bebelle. I've been trying for the last few days." It's the truth. Oliver has gone completely off the grid, and I know the same can be said about Brody, even though I'll try to hunt him down later.

"I want out of this house," she moans and hands me the few possessions she has here. "I don't know where he put my phone."

"Who cares?" I grab her things. "I'll get you a new one."

I lead her out of the room and find Caine down at the foot of the stairs.

"Ready, ma petite?" His jaw is tight, and anger is still radiating off of him in waves.

"Yes." Her smile is wide, but her eyes are sad.

I have a bag of frozen peas pressed to my cheek, and a duo of glaring assholes in front of me.

"You honestly thought it was a good idea to leave her there?" Cooper screams.

"The first time I saw her, it wasn't that bad, and yes, I agreed with it. The second time she wanted to stay." I sound pathetic, even to myself.

"I should've known he would do this to her," Caine growls. "We are just as much to blame for letting her stay."

"You realize she's an adult, and she needs to make her own decisions?" I snap. "You're treating her like a child. This woman killed her own father to save Brody. Do you think that's someone who wanted to be away from him?"

They both glare at me, but their lack of response tells me they know I'm right.

"Where could he have gone?" Caine paces again.

"Maybe he skipped the country?" Cooper suggests.

"No," I disagree. "He's preparing for a showdown with Oliver. I can feel it."

"Is there any way both of them can come out of this alive?" Cooper asks.

"I don't think so," Caine huffs, then sits on the couch. "If Oliver doesn't kill Brody, then Kennedy will kill his own son. We know there's no love lost between them. If Brody gets the chance, he will kill Oliver, and he'll do it purely for fun."

Yeah, he would. Brody has always loved the game of cat and mouse. It feeds his inner monster and soothes his tumultuous soul. Then there's the love he has for torture. He calls it an art and loves to practice his skills whenever he gets the chance.

"So we wait around until the showdown?" I ask, and Caine throws me a dark look.

"Fuck, no." He grins, and it transforms his face into something sinister. "If Brody is going to die, I'm going to make sure it's by my hand."

Well, fuck.

KAILEY·HIMARI

TWENTY-NINE

It feels good to be in my bed, wrapped in my blankets, and between two men I love with my whole heart. Cooper is to my left with his arm thrown over his eyes and breathing deeply, and then Caine is to my right, his face lined in anger, even in sleep.

I have to use the bathroom, but I don't want to disturb them. They look completely exhausted, and I know it's because I haven't been home.

"Stop wiggling," Caine groans.

"I have to pee," I whisper.

"Did you lose the ability to use the toilet along with your common sense in that house?" At least he doesn't sound so angry today.

"I didn't want to wake you." I roll my eyes and sit up. "I should call Kimmy too."

"Yeah, she's been annoying as all hell," Cooper mutters from my left. "She just didn't believe you'd want to be alone with Brody. Maybe we should've fucking listened to her."

"Good morning." I lean over and kiss his cheek. "I really need to pee."

On the way to the bathroom, I text Kimmy.

Me: Hey. I'm home.

Her reply is instant, and I can feel the disdain through her words.

Kimmy: Call me now.

I bite the bullet and call her while I'm pissing on the fucking toilet.

"You better have a good explanation." She sounds angry.

"I was kidnapped and held against my will?" It's the truth.

"Seriously, Kailey! You fucking had me worried." Kimmy rarely swears. "What the heck happened?"

"I needed to just spend some time alone with Brody and figure out how to be with his friends while having a friendship with him." Ha! What a crock of shit!

"And?" She sounds a little better. "How did that work out for you?"

"It didn't. There's no middle ground for us." I couldn't hold back the sadness in my voice if I tried.

"Aw, boo. I'm sorry. I know what he meant to you at one time."

"How was your Christmas? Tell me Henry got you somethin' worth a fortune," I gush, trying to change the subject.

"Oh! Girl!" she squeals. "My man proposed to me in front of my mama and daddy! Got right down on one knee and everything!"

"Oh, my god!" I jump up off the toilet. "Oh, my god!"

"You need to see this ring. I can barely lift my gosh darn hand!" Her excitement about the engagement has taken the heat off my entire ordeal, and I couldn't be more thankful.

"I'm a bridesmaid, right?"

"Boo, you are my maid of honor! Even though you left me in the dark for days." Well, hell, that went downhill.

"I'm sorry, Kimmy."

"I understand why you did it, but don't you think your heart deserves happiness after everything?" she asks.

"Yeah," I agree solemnly. Why then does it feel like it was ripped out of my chest?

"How is your daddy taking all of this? Multiple boyfriends and all."

Fuck, this is something I didn't expect. How the hell do I answer this? Maybe partial truths.

"Kimmy, remember I told you Papa had a drinking problem and went to rehab for a little while?"

"Yes, of course. I commend him for fighting his demons," she praises. He *was* a fucking demon.

"Well, it was more than that. He was also addicted to

drugs and was supposed to stay longer at the facility. I was told last week he left of his own accord, and I can't locate him."

"Oh, my gosh!" she gasps. "Boo, are you okay? Did you call the police?"

At the mention of the police, my heart jumps and trips over every fucking rib in my chest.

"Yes, they're looking for him."

"Did you want to come and stay with me? Mama wouldn't mind. We could have sleepovers and prepare for our New Year's ball."

Right, the fucking ball.

"I have the guys with me. I'm okay. We need to go shopping though," I sigh.

"I have my dress, but we definitely need to go for you. It's masked!"

Even better. "All right, tomorrow?"

"Yes!" she squeals.

I finally placate her enough and get off the phone. I glance in the mirror and cringe at the greenish/yellow bruises lining my throat. Looks like a turtleneck tomorrow, and hopefully they're gone by New Year's Eve. If not, I should buy some heavy-duty foundation.

"Everything okay with Kimmy?" Cooper asks as soon as I step out of the bathroom.

"She and Henry are engaged." I smile.

Caine is still sleeping while Cooper is propped up and looking at his phone.

"Really?" He grins at me, and then suddenly his face is

serious again. "One day you will be too."

"Oh, yeah?" I tease as I crawl back up the bed between them. "And how would that work?"

"Obviously, you would marry me. I was the mastermind behind this whole thing." His grin is wide and contagious.

"Fuck off," Caine's gruff voice cuts into our playful moment. "She's going to be a Leblanc."

Well, I can see this is going to be a future problem. I roll my eyes and snuggle back down into the covers.

"Maybe I'll just stay a Richard," I murmur as I press my ass into Caine, and wrap my arm around Cooper's waist. Although, the name Richard no longer has any appeal for me.

Caine's big arm comes around my waist as his face presses into the back of my neck.

"Go back to sleep," he rasps.

"You looked so good in red at Georgina's party!" Kimmy coos as we peruse the racks of gowns. "Has anyone seen her around?"

It's gotten out that Georgina had a huge fight with her mother about an affair, and she ran away from home. Her mother was the one to call the police when she was alerted to Georgina's bank account being emptied. I thank every angel watching us that they had a huge blowout about my father the same night Brody got a hold of her.

I really don't want to be here, I don't want to go to this ball, and I really want to be curled up in my bed. I owe this to

Kimmy, and that's the only reason I'm here.

"Nothing so far." I shrug. "You know her. She's so dramatic. She'll come running back at some point."

I've become an expert liar.

I find a black lace, open back gown. I pull it off the rack and gasp at the weight. It's heavy and luxurious.

"I think I found one," I call out, and Kimmy comes rushing over.

"Well, heck, boo, I think you did." She claps and runs off to find a matching mask.

I would rather ring in the New Year with all my guys at home. I still haven't heard anything from Oliver, and Zeke is still hard at work trying to trace Brody. If I could just get a hold of Oliver, I would try to convince him to come home. We could figure everything else out.

"I booked us a spa during the day on New Year's Eve, we'll get our hair and nails done." She pointedly looks at my grown-out highlights.

"Yes, ma'am." I roll my eyes.

Tonight is my first day back at the restaurant. Thankfully they kept me on even after missing two scheduled shifts. I wish I could be home with the guys catching up and just relaxing, but I need this job to at least contribute something.

"Now, let's go have some lunch, and you fill me in on all things Brody," Kimmy suggests as she slips her arm in mine. "I asked them to deliver everything to your house, along with masks for your men."

Great… Time for more lies.

ZEKE

THIRTY

"Are you absolutely fucking sure?" Caine stands looking just as shocked as I'm feeling.

"Yes, strangled to death," I confirm.

"Do you think Oliver...?" Cooper trails off, and we all stand in collective silence.

Thankfully Kailey is at work tonight, because I really wouldn't know how to explain the shit-storm I've stumbled across.

"It hasn't hit the media yet, just internal within the family," I tell them. "Maybe Oliver will bring his ass back, and we can find out exactly what happened."

"Something doesn't feel right." Caine presses his fingers to his mouth and paces again.

He's right, it doesn't. This is sudden, and it's going to cause a fucking uproar throughout all the families.

"Is there any way this is bullshit? Something they're saying to cause a distraction for something bigger?" Cooper asks.

"If that was the case, they would have alerted the authorities or the media," I interject. "What distraction could they cause by keeping it within the family?"

"True," he mutters.

"No, he's dead. There's no denying that. The question is who did it?" Caine says.

"And I think we need to prepare ourselves for something big to go down," I tell them as I widen the image on my screen.

Kennedy Ballon is laying in a lavish, clawfoot tub, as naked as the day he was born, and wearing only a set of dark purple bruises around his neck. Bruises that looked very similar to the ones around Kailey's a few days ago.

"Oliver has had many years and opportunities to kill his father. Why would he do it now?" Cooper asks.

"I don't think he did. This screams our boy all over it," Caine growls.

"If Brody did this," I say while pointing at the screen. "Then he's just started a fucking war."

"A war would give us a fighting chance," Cooper groans. "This is Armageddon."

"Zeke." Caine looks at me. "We really need to find Brody or Oliver; this shit is about to get messy."

"Someone call my name?"

We all jump up at the sound of Oliver's voice as he steps into the room. He looks haggard, unshaved, and sleep deprived.

"Bro!" Cooper yells. "Did you kill our brother?"

"No, I got sidetracked and found out my father was killed instead." He walks straight to the cabinet and takes out the bourbon. "I offered Brody an out. If he leaves the country, I will let him go."

"The first target you didn't kill?" Caine asks.

"How do you know I killed each target?" He takes the cap off the bottle and takes a few gulps. "Things have changed now that *he's* dead." He points at the screen with his father's picture.

"How so?" Cooper watches him closely.

"My brothers can never hold me to my contract, because it was signed with that sadistic fucker." He tips back the bottle again. "Now he's dead, and my contract goes with him."

"They are going to think it was you." Cooper narrows his eyes. "Won't they try to kill you?"

"They know it's not me. When that shit happened, I was getting drunk with my older brother."

"Shit," Caine mutters, obviously thinking the same thing I am. Brody just dipped us all in hot water.

"Kailey is at work?" Oliver asks as he puts the bottle away.

"She's been trying to get a hold of you," Caine growls.

"Can't take the chance my brothers find out about her. Any connection is a weakness, and each of you knows that." He stalks out of the room, and we hear the front door open then shut.

"We need to find Brody." Cooper stares at me.

"Yeah." I nod. "Easier said than done."

"How the fuck did he pull this off?" Caine continues to

prowl as I tap away on the darknet.

"Why do we want to save him?" Cooper falls to the couch. "Look what he did to Kailey."

"Because he's not well, because he's our brother no matter what, and we need him," I answer him.

"I want to kill him, but Zeke is right. We made a pact a long time ago, and we know the demons he fights daily."

"You're right." Cooper scrubs his hand down his face. "I just hate him right now."

"I know." I nod. I do too.

"The New Year's Eve party is going to be a problem. We will be out in the open where everyone can see us. Easy to be picked off one by one," Caine fumes.

"It's also an excellent opportunity to see the other families out in the open," I add.

Kimmy picked the biggest function in New Orleans to go to. I doubt she knew it, but this is a high society function, and the big families always make an appearance. This year we will represent ours.

The only thing making me apprehensive is this year they made it a masked ball. Faces are partially obscured or even fully, it'll work in our favor, sure, but also in theirs. Should make for an interesting night.

"I need to go pick up sha." Cooper gets up. "Maybe from now on, someone is with her at all times, even while she works."

"Yeah," I agree with him.

We are no longer free to roam as we did. We'll be hunted and killed off one by one until one of us confesses to that murder. No one kills a king pin without declaring war, and Brody just created World War III.

"We need to sober up Oliver; he can give us inside information and help us with traveling in pairs," Caine thinks out loud.

Brody better be somewhere safe, because I can't worry about him and keep a proper eye on everything around me. I will be expected to trace, track, and follow all movements. This is my expertise, but none of the others will know how to handle Brody should they come face-to-face. He won't be himself, and the monster is not something to fuck with.

I know he's not medicated right now because he needs to think strategically, and that just means his instincts belong to the monster too.

Instincts that fight without thought of flight.

KAILEYHIMARI

THIRTY-ONE

The restaurant is empty tonight, with just a few couples coming in for dinner. The holidays are meant to be spent with families, unless the family you have is all dead. Then I guess go to your nearest greasy restaurant and order a fucking burger.

"Kailey," the owner calls out from the back. "After these few are done, we'll head out. No need to stay late tonight."

"Sounds good," I call back and pull the bags out of the garbage bins. Might as well start the closing chores.

I gather up the few bags and head through the back, opening the back door for the dumpster. I toss the bags inside as I hear someone's throat clear, not just anyone's.

"Why would you want to work in this grease pit?" His pretentious voice drips with disgust.

"Because I had a father who left me with a mountain of debt, and few skills to boast about," I snap back.

"I don't know about that." He chuckles. "You can ride dick pretty well. That's a needed skill."

"Are you okay, Brody?" I ask as he steps out of the shadows.

His eyes look empty again and his voice is hollow.

"I'm good." He nods. "Are you okay?"

"Yes," I whisper, then I shake my head. "No."

"Miss me?" His voice is taunting but holds a note of something else in it. Hope maybe, or I'm just hoping it does.

"It's complicated," I answer truthfully. "I want you safe. Come home with me, and we can help you."

"I have everything planned out, Kails. I just needed to make sure you were okay." He kicks at a tin can. "That you were staying strong."

"I survived your brother, and then I survived you, Brody. I'm strong." I lift my chin and glare at him.

"That's what I needed to hear." He steps forward and flicks my nose. "I'll see you around."

"Wait!" I call to his retreating back. "When will you be home?"

He lifts his hand up but continues to walk away. I watch him until I can't see him any longer, and then I continue to watch the dark shadows a little longer. I head back inside, and my phone pings in my apron. I pull it out and swipe open the screen, hoping to see Brody's name.

Cooper: I'm waiting outside for you. Let me know when you're done.

Me: Perfect! Getting off early.

The register needs to be closed after the last two people pay. I call out my goodbyes to the owner and head outside. I see Cooper's Wrangler idling in the lot, his face is illuminated inside by the light of his cell phone, and he looks up as if sensing me.

He quickly jumps out of the Jeep, looking around as he jogs to my side.

"Hey?" I give him a confused look. He's acting a little overprotective.

"Hi, sha." He gathers me up in his arms and presses a kiss to my forehead. "Mmm, is that French fries I smell?"

I groan and shove him away. "I'm probably shiny as hell too, huh?"

"Nah." His grin is wide and those dimples flash at me, making me swoon.

We get into the Wrangler, and he looks at me with a serious face. "He's home."

I nod. "Yeah, I…"

"And his father is dead."

"What?" I gasp.

"Kennedy Ballon was found strangled in his bathtub at home."

He's not talking about Brody, he's talking about Oliver, and that means Oliver hasn't been trying to kill Brody. I don't know why, but I decided that not knowing that Brody has been around is for the best. Yes, I am protecting the man that tried to destroy me.

"Is Oliver at the house?" I ask.

"No, he left soon after he showed up. He seems like maybe he's been drinking a lot."

"It's time Oliver and I have a talk about him avoiding me," I mutter, watching the passing streetlamps as Cooper takes me home.

When we step inside, I can feel the tension like a suffocating smoke, clogging the air, and seeping into our pores. Caine steps out of the family room and strides up to me.

"We need to talk."

"Yeah." I nod and follow him inside the family room.

Zeke is sitting on the couch and tapping away on two separate laptops. He barely looks up to acknowledge me.

"Coop told me Oliver is back," I tell them, and Zeke finally looks away.

"He is, and his father was found dead earlier today."

"He told me that, too." I nod.

"We think Brody did it," Caine says to me.

"Why?" I frown.

Zeke turns one of his laptops around, and I see an obese, naked man, sprawled out in his tub, and water all over the floor.

"Okay." I look up at Caine. "Why do you think Brody did it?"

"His throat, sha," Cooper whispers as he comes up behind me.

"Oh." I see the markings on the man's throat, eerily similar to the ones fading on mine.

"Kennedy Ballon was an evil man." I shrug. "He did this town a favor."

"No, bebelle." Zeke shakes his head. "He has started a war, and now the families will be watching each other, waiting for someone to pounce. We have to stay safe and always be in pairs."

"One of us will be with you at all times." Caine nods.

"Sometimes maybe two," Cooper breathes into my ear, and I shiver at the thought.

"I need a shower," I groan, and start up the stairs.

"Need a back washer?" Cooper playfully calls out.

I want to tell him yes. I want to be ready to be intimate with them again, but I can't. It has nothing to do with the trauma and everything to do with the fact that I don't want to replace Brody just yet. I know I'm a fucking loser.

"Rain check!" I call out.

The shower runs cold by the time I shut it off. I can't stop thinking about Brody, and whether or not he really killed that man… Oliver's father. Then there's Oliver himself, disappearing and then reappearing like I haven't been trying to get a hold of him. He still hasn't tried to contact me.

I dress in a comfy pair of pajamas and head back down with the guys. They are right where I left them, only now they're arguing about motives and power.

"Brody did it because Oliver was after him," Zeke says.

"No, Brody has always wanted Kennedy dead," Caine argues.

"Actually, I think Kennedy also wanted Brody dead," I cut in, and they all fall silent to look at me. "He tried to make my papa do it, and when he failed, he called in his Terminator son."

When they don't say anything else, I continue. "Look, he would never stop trying to kill Brody. So the only way to make it stop was to kill him first." I shrug. "Makes sense."

"What happened to our sweet-as-all-heck girl?" Cooper teases.

"She grew a fucking backbone." I shrug again and head into the kitchen.

I look out the back door toward the gazebo and wonder if Brody is still collecting petals even though I have his box. Has he been by here the last few days? Does *he* miss me?

The wind blows the vines as a few of the petals break off and catch on to the breeze. Tomorrow, I am calling in a landscaper to come clean that tree up. I'll do it for Mama, but I'll also do it for Brody.

But mostly for me, as a reminder to live vibrant and free.

ZEKE

THIRTY-TWO

Something is different about Kailey.

Am I stupid for making such an observation when the reason is so clearly screaming at me? Yeah. I want to say she's different because Brody tortured her and held her captive, but I feel like that's not it. She's acting heartbroken, not soul broken.

Brody somehow made her fall in love with him, or she just never really stopped. She's not really moping around the house, but I can see she gets wistful when she looks at certain things. I want to ask her what's going on, but I feel like I'm intruding on her trying to mend her heart.

The others haven't noticed, although Cooper has voiced that she hasn't really wanted to touch them since she's been back. All I can hope for is that time helps her heal or Brody gets his shit together and works it out with us.

I'm sitting on my bike outside of Oliver's at five in the morning because I found something interesting about his family.

I walk up to his front door and ring the bell. A few moments later, I hear the door unlock, but the door doesn't open. Okay, then. I open the door and look inside.

Oliver is standing across from the door, leaning against the wall with his arms crossed over his chest. "It's early as fuck," he growls, and I notice the dark bags under his eyes.

"You sleeping, man?"

"What do you want?" He rolls his eyes.

"Why haven't you been by to see Kailey?"

"Probably because I doubt she'd want to see me after I tried to hunt down her newest boyfriend and kill him," he snarls.

"Brody wasn't—"

"You don't know shit," he cuts me off, then heads farther into the house.

I close the door and follow behind him. "So tell me," I say to his back.

"When I went to see him, he was smug." His eyes are hard and filled with rage. "She wants him, even after all he did to her these last few years."

"I told you they had history. It's not our place to judge what they have." I try to defend both of them.

"Isn't it?" he asks. "Aren't we all in this together?"

"We respect each other, we help each other, and we protect each other. Not anywhere in there should we judge each other."

"I got her text messages, begging me not to kill him even after everything he did to her… What his brother did to her," he spits out.

I get what he's saying. I honestly do. It's a hard pill to swallow, but it's not for us to swallow.

"Her decision." I shrug. "She'd do the same for any one of us. Stop avoiding her and talk to her."

He looks down at his feet, and I can sense he's hurt; I think maybe he saw what I'm seeing in the aftermath of Kailey loving Brody.

"I found something last night," I tell him as I pull my bag off my shoulder. "Your brother Cameron has been up to some shit."

"Like what?" He pushes off the counter and pulls out a chair at the table.

I sit down and pull out my laptop. "He's put a hit out on Brody, not to kill, but to bring in for questioning."

"Fuck," he groans, and I know I was right.

"He's going to be hitting your weak spots. Maybe this one was a little more like your father than you originally thought."

I figured he'd want to grab Brody for information on his father's death, and then information pertaining to Oliver. We all know Brody was the information gatherer in our group, and that was never a secret. If they get Brody, I am confident he wouldn't spill anything he didn't want to, but I can't guarantee one of those things is Kailey. I don't know how important she is to him. I thought I had an idea, but fuck… I was wrong.

"You're worried if they get him, he'll spill about Kailey." He reads me like an open book.

"Yeah."

"Then clearly, my staying away isn't such a bad idea," he retorts.

I slide a burner phone over to him and give him a pointed look.

"Call her. Talk it out, because she loves you."

"I love her too." He exhales with a huff.

"I know. It's the only reason I'm here." I grin at him. "Now, what's your plan?"

After my talk with Oliver, I'm more worried about Brody's safety, and figuring out his whereabouts is now a priority. According to Oliver, his family will try to exploit him further to gain his skills in the long run. That means they would grab Brody intending to torture him for the information he possesses, and Brody is notorious for his gathering of information, especially through torturous methods.

That's exactly how he has gained most of his information about the Ballons. He's grabbed some of their higher-level grunts, then tortured them with pleasure. Now the Ballons want to return the favor. The bounty on Brody's head has doubled overnight, and I fear someone else will find him before we do.

The house is quiet when I get in. They are all probably still sleeping while I do the legwork to keep us all safe and sound. I roll my eyes and head for the kitchen; I need coffee and a lot of it. I make a beeline straight to the coffee machine and prep it.

"Where did you go?" Caine's voice startles me from behind.

I turn and find him sitting at the table, watching me closely, and with his signature frown on his face.

"I went to see Oliver."

"Why would you do that alone? We don't know what kind of mindset he's in," Caine scolds.

"He's hurt about Kailey deserting y'all, her many attempts to call and text him to save Brody's life, and he's worried she's choosing him over us," I explain.

"Us?" Caine's smile transforms his usually granite face.

"Yeah." I nod. "Us."

"I'm glad you've come around, bro."

I shrug, and turn back to the coffee machine, busying myself to avoid getting into a conversation with Caine about feelings and shit.

"Coffee," Cooper moans as he stumbles into the kitchen.

"Good. Now that you're both here. I need to discuss what me and Oliver came up with." I let the machine percolate and sit at the table. "Brody now has a bounty on his head for half a million dollars. He is to be captured by any means possible, except death."

"They want him alive, obviously." Caine nods.

"Because he has a way of digging up information anywhere," Cooper chimes in.

"Exactly." I nod. "We know his loyalty lies with us three right here, but would that extend to Oliver? Or Kailey?"

"And Kailey is Oliver's weak point," Caine surmises. "They would have a way to rope him back in as The Teacher."

"That's what I'm thinking," I agree. "Why would they just let their very best assassin leave the organization? It doesn't matter who signed that contract, they will still make it valid."

"We need to find Brody first," Caine growls. "Where the fuck would the prick go?"

"I have searched every Landry property that I know of. There hasn't been any recent movement. He didn't take a vehicle, and he has yet to withdraw money or use a credit card."

"What about surveillance activity around town?" Cooper interjects.

"It's harder to catch facial recognition than it is to find a vehicle. I've tried, but the scanners have picked up only potential matches. Some could be him, but it's hard to tell," I shrug.

"Do you think he would try to reach out to Kailey? Or maybe he's still planning something against Oliver?" Caine suggests.

"I don't know about reaching out to Kailey. I would assume him leaving her alone deems her useless to him, and I think him taking out Kennedy Ballon was his attempt to stop the assassination," I tell them.

"I don't know if it was about him stopping the assassination." Caine rubs his chin. "More of him making a statement, if you ask me."

"I agree," Cooper adds. "He knows Ballon has four sons. They would obviously carry on his wishes."

"What the fuck is he doing?" Caine mutters.

That's what I would like to know. Where the fuck is Brody?

BRODY

THIRTY-THREE

The leaves sway in the breeze above my head, and the air is holding a slight chill tonight. Sleeping outside, feeling the surrounding life, and becoming one with my inner peace has been motherfucking torture. Every fucking chirp of a bird, buzz of an insect, and the shuffle of a person's feet on the pavement, makes me want to slice open throats.

I have no choice. I have to be here to make sure she's safe, and I have to monitor who may come around here at odd hours of the day or night. If anyone is killing Kailey-Himari, it's me.

The petals shake, and some break away from the vine to slowly float down around my head and body. I remember when this tree was planted, and the day is still vivid in my mind. Sara was sick with a cold, and both Kailey and I were watching TV with her. Charles came into the family room, asking her to join him in the backyard. At first, she declined, saying she was really feeling under the weather, but he somehow convinced her, and we all followed behind him.

I remember thinking the so-called tree looked more like a twig sticking out of the ground, and the little purple flowers were sparse, but Sara cried with joy. She explained to Kailey and me that she had one very similar in Japan, and that it grew to be big and beautiful. I didn't believe her then, but looking at it now, I wish she could see her prophecy come true.

I tried to stay in the shadows, blend in and keep an eye on Kailey. Then I watched her coming out of the backdoor of that restaurant, and I just had to talk to her, hear her voice. I've become slightly obsessed, and my need to be near her is too strong to deny now. With that need comes the desire to claim her and kill her in equal parts. My mind becomes foggy with images of her sucking my dick, then morphs into ones of me strangling her to death.

The floor of gazebo is hard, but this is the perfect place to hide in plain sight, and if Kailey had at least two brain cells in her fucking head, she would've figured it out by now. I gave her a fucking box of these petals for fuck's sake. It doesn't matter whether or not she finds me, I've just disrupted a delicate truce, and New Orleans is about to be spun on its head. Well, the underbelly of it.

By now, I'm sure Zeke has tried every trick he has to find me. Cell phone trace, credit card trail, face recognition, and tracking my car, but I know how to avoid all that. Then there's The Teacher. He's back home now, and I can see he's also trying to lie low, thinking the death of his father releases their hold on him, but it's fucking laughable how stupid that is. I need him to stay away from Kailey, and so far, he's done that.

I just need to hold out here for a few more days, and then everything I have planned will be done. It won't be easy and there will be sacrifice, but the end will be worth it.

desecrated ESSENCE

KAILEY HIMARI

THIRTY-FOUR

I am in some kind of funk that I can't seem to shake. I'm tired, like bone-deep exhausted. I don't sleep well, and food just isn't appealing. Even kissing my boyfriends has become weird as I have yet to be intimate with any of them. Am I that far gone because of Brody? He punched a hole through my chest, ripped out my heart and fucking tore it to shreds, but I think he might own every single frayed piece.

Or maybe he damaged me beyond repair, and now my sick, little soul craves the depravity. Regardless of what it is, I think about him constantly, wondering about every *what if* there is, and feeling complete and utter despair for the four other men in my life. The men that have treated me like the most precious thing in their lives, the men that protect me, and the ones that return my love without restraint.

What is wrong with me? The stress and constant questioning of my feelings have disrupted my life. I need a resolution, and I need it soon.

Brody came by the restaurant. Does that mean he's watching me somehow? Is he trailing my whereabouts? I need to talk to him again because I need to hear him say how much he doesn't love me. I need him to stomp all those small, frayed pieces of my heart into dust, just like those petals.

Just like those petals… The petals!

I run upstairs to Mama and Papa's bedroom, and press my body against the glass door, trying to see through the vines into the gazebo. Could he be in there? Would he really continue to come back every day? There's really only one way to find out, and yet I can't seem to force my feet to move. Even though I need him to break me further, it doesn't mean I *want* him to.

The breeze is blowing through the vines this evening, and I am standing here just waiting to get a glimpse inside. The landscaper came by today, and when he saw the state of the tree, he promised to be back tomorrow with the proper equipment and the men. So for now, the unruly branches taunt me with their complete coverage.

I need to go see.

I grab a sweater from my room and rush to the kitchen.

"Who lit a fire under your ass?" Caine calls out from the family room. They've been holed up in that room all day, searching for the very man I ache for.

"Just want to sit in the fresh air," I answer. "Is the backyard okay?" I watch as Zeke and Cooper look at each other while Caine stares into my face. No one answers, and the room falls deathly silent. "I need to feel close to Mama," I whisper, hating myself for using my grief as a tool to get my way.

"Ten minutes, and then we come check on you," Caine answers, and the other two nod.

"Okay." I smile.

I hurry outside and panic; I need all of those ten minutes to count… If he's even here. There is a blanket of purple petals in front of me as I run to the gazebo. Ten minutes! I try to remind myself, but my feet are stuck.

What would I say? Can I really survive another round with Brody?

I have been through worse. So much worse, I can do this.

I close my eyes and step through the vines. I stand still in the entryway, feeling the vines brush my back, and their strong perfume permeating the small place.

Please be here.

I open my eyes and frantically search the small area, my eyes adjusting and my heart beating. Nothing, and no one is here. I sit on the bench and exhale the hope that shouldn't exist. How did I convince myself of this? Have I truly driven myself crazy?

I drop my head into my hands and hear the rustle of the vines as the breeze blows by again. Stupid, *stupid,* Kailey.

"Took you long enough." His voice, like honey, slowly seeps through me and settles inside of my soul.

I lift my head and see him sitting across from me on the bench.

"Have you been staying here?" Why am I asking these mundane questions when I care nothing for the answers?

"Yes." His brow raises, the slight movement has me flying off the bench and straight into his arms.

Brody's legs open, and I plow between them, wrapping him up and pressing his head to my chest. His scent, like something musky and unique, floods my nose, and I breathe in contentment at its familiarity. His arms come up and slowly wrap around my waist.

"Vibrant and free," I whisper.

"You always were, Kails."

"Are you hungry?" I pull back to hold his face between my hands. "Cold?"

"I ate and I'm fine." He pulls my hands off his face and presses them against my sides.

"Brody, come inside, please," I beg him. "They're looking for you."

"I can't." He shakes his head. "I need you to do me a favor, though."

"Okay." I nod.

"I need you to remember the pain I caused you. Remember how much I remind you of my brother." He's saying all the things I needed to hear, yet they don't have the effect I was hoping for.

"I can't." I shake my head. "I think there's something wrong with me."

"I'm letting you near me, touching me, and talking to me because we were once best friends, but don't take any of this for more than what it is. I pity you because of what you suffered in your life, but that's it."

"Keep going." I feel my heart hardening at his words, and a familiar anger covers the despair.

"You deserted me, and now I will see you as nothing more than a traitor. I will one day return when all of this is over to kill you."

"Almost there," I grit through my teeth.

He stands, looming over me, and sneering down his nose at me. "You are damaged goods, and I would never consider you good enough for the Landry name." And that just locked everything into place. I turn on my heel and look at him over my shoulder.

"I would watch your back, Landry."

Then I'm running across my backyard with tears dripping off my chin and my heart in shambles. This is exactly what I needed, so why does it feel like I was hoping for something different? Something completely impossible?

Brody Landry is dead to me now.

KAILEY HIMARI

THIRTY-FIVE

"Boo!" Kimmy squeals and hops a little on the spot. "You look ravishing!"

I look down at the black satin and lace gown, running my hands over the intricate design. Thankfully, hiding the carved initials over my breast that still tingles now and then.

"So do you, Kimmy." She's wearing a golden gown that shimmers in the light.

I still had some bruising on my throat, so I left my hair down and covered the rest with a heavy foundation. The dress is simple in design but rich in detail. The black lace overlay is heavy and regal. The straps are thin around my shoulders, and then the back opens up, hitting just above my ass crack. I am the dress version of business in the front and party in the back.

I paired it with a high stiletto heel in a matte-black finish, and I'm praying not to die tonight. My hair and makeup are pretty muted since I figured I would be behind a partial mask most of the night. I put on the black lace mask, and it fits perfectly with my dress.

"Am I too over the top?" Kimmy does a twirl, and I am momentarily stunned by the shimmering fabric.

"No," I breathe.

Kimmy looks like true royalty. Her gown is a sweetheart neckline that forms a corset top, and then the dress blooms out all the way to her feet. This is the golden version of Cinderella's gown, and I am envious that she can pull it off. She tied her hair back with golden clips, letting some curls cascade down her back. Her makeup is dramatic. Smokey eyes, and a bright red lip, then her mask looks like a golden starburst around her eyes. She looks like a goddess.

I am finally feeling a little like myself today. It's taken a few days, but when I woke up this morning, I took my first full breath. My head has completely recovered from my temporary lapse in judgment, and now my heart has finally caught up.

Brody Landry is now my former best friend and tormentor; he no longer holds any special place inside of me. That boy I once loved has died along with the hope of ever being anything more. Thanks to him, I can face anything.

"Let's go shock all your men," she giggles. "And mine too."

Henry was bombarded by Cooper as soon as he came through the door, and the two have formed a bond. Both being quarterbacks helps a lot. Caine and Zeke are still trying to locate Brody, and I don't dare tell them he's in the backyard. Out of sight, out of mind.

Oliver has been texting me, and I get late-night phone calls from him. He explained his absence and promised me it's not for much longer. I miss him, and I want him to come home to me. Unfortunately, he can't come with us tonight.

We make our way down the stairs and sway into the family room. Kimmy's dress is so large and puffy, she has to push her way through the doorway.

"Ahem," she clears her throat, and all of them look up.

"That's my baby, y'all." Henry jumps up off the couch and rushes to Kimmy. "My princess."

"Sha." Cooper's awed voice steals away my attention from my best friend and her cooing fiancé. "You look like an angel."

"A dark forbidden one," Caine says, advancing toward me.

His fingers grab my waist and pull me in as Cooper comes up behind me, brushing my hair aside. One set of lips hit the nape of my neck, and another to the corner of my mouth.

"Move out of the way," Zeke growls from behind Caine.

Caine moves aside with a chuckle, and then Zeke's cushion lips are pressing against mine. Cooper's exploring my neck, and Zeke is exploring my mouth.

"Henry," Kimmy breathes. "I want one."

I can't hold in my snort, and Zeke lifts his head with a laugh.

"Allons," Henry says as he drags his fiancée out of the room. "Don't give her any ideas, y'all."

The guys went all out on a stretch limo and buckets of champagne. They pop a bottle outside, and Kimmy giggles when it foams over Caine's hand. I decline the glass since drinking has never been something I've enjoyed.

Kimmy and Henry pile into the limo just as Caine grabs

my hand and holds me back. "Make sure you never leave our side tonight," he tells me. "Bathroom breaks are always with one of us."

"Okay." I nod, then lean up to kiss his cheek.

I know they are nervous and worried about what will happen tonight when all the most important men in New Orleans are gathered in one spot. I just want to have one night to enjoy myself and my men without the added worry of being killed. Is that really too much to ask?

I get into the limo, and the guys jump in as well. All have black tuxes and masks, the only thing differentiating them is their hair and body types. To most, they will blend into the crowd. To me, they shine like beacons of pure sex. Maybe tonight will be the night I get my fucking groove back.

I squirm a bit in my seat at the thought, and Caine grasps my thigh. He knows what I'm thinking, he always knows. Cooper chuckles as he catches on, and Zeke licks his lips with anticipation.

"Temptation really is the Devil," Kimmy mutters.

"Is his name Henry?" Henry looks at her with his brow raised. "Because that's the only temptation you're gettin'."

I snort into my hand, and the others aren't too far behind, their laughter filling the interior.

"Y'all are gonna get me in trouble," Kimmy mutters, and we all let loose another laugh.

The venue for this ball is the Elms Mansion and Gardens. It's a historical site for us here in NOLA, and it's still run by the descendants of one of the original owners. The estate was built in 1862, and the place just exudes class and charm. I've heard so many great things about the events held there, and even though I could very well be targeted tonight, I'm fucking excited.

We pull up to the front, and I see a long line of stretch limos. The place is sparkling with lights, and I can hear a string band in the background. We pull up, and the door is opened by two security guards.

"Gentlemen, we are doing pat downs tonight, and ladies kindly open your clutches," one of them says.

I really hope Cooper and Caine aren't carrying.

"Is there a bomb threat or something?" Henry asks as the guard pats him down.

"No, sir, just standard procedure."

"Especially when the place is full of mobsters," Cooper grumbles under his breath.

We all get the pat down and purse check out of the way, then make our way inside. The place is absolutely gorgeous. All handmade moldings, original wood panel floorings, and the lamps on the walls sing of the 1800's. I want to live here.

"Boo, let's hit the bar." Kimmy grabs my arm.

"Kimmy!" I say in a whisper. "We are not legal."

"Gosh, darn it, Kailey. If you don't loosen up one of these days, I am going to spank you."

"What?" I rear back with a laugh.

"This is high society. If we're here, they don't bother with ID's. Drink, but keep it classy, and people turn the other cheek. Got it, sugar?"

"Got it," I giggle, and let her drag me to the bar.

I notice Caine is right behind us, and I breathe a sigh of relief knowing they will keep me protected. Having them here with me all together really sets my soul at ease. I just miss Oliver, and my heart is trying to remind me of a certain pair of icy blues, but I shut that down real quick.

"Not too much to drink tonight, ma petite," Caine says quietly behind me.

I nod, knowing he'll see the movement, and follow Kimmy in the queue to the bar. It looks like Kimmy is expecting to kick loose tonight. That means I really need to stay sober and keep an eye on her. One glass of champagne will do for the night.

Once we have our flutes in hand, we make our way over to a table designed straight out of a magazine. The centerpieces are beautiful lilies with tiny LED lights twinkling around them.

"Let's take some pictures." Kimmy grabs my hand, and I'm being hauled off again. This time, Zeke is close behind.

I haven't really seen Zeke in a suit and tie, except for Georgina's birthday party, but he wasn't really on my radar then. He looks deadly, like a panther, coiled and oozing with dark hunger. I fucking want him. My stomach quivers, and my pussy dampens my panties. Welcome back, you horny slut.

Zeke is on camera duty, taking pictures of us as I imagine his cock, large and full of piercings, driving into me. Okay, time to get his ass alone and sate this hunger of mine.

"I need a bathroom break," I tell Kimmy, and watch as she pouts. "Girl, there are enough pictures to make an album already."

"Fine!" she huffs. "I'll get Henry."

I watch her push through the crowd to find her husband to be.

"Bathroom?" I look at Zeke, imagining his cock choking me.

He scans my face, and his eyes darken with desire. "Yeah."

We're doing this.

I grab his hand and skate through the crowd, looking for a private room. I find the entrance to the back patio and see it's less populated. The beautiful gazebo near the back looks perfect. Outside is our thing, after all.

"My bebelle loves to get her pussy beat the fuck up outside, huh?" he whispers at my back.

My thighs clench at his words and the gravelly sound of his voice. I need him inside of me. This sudden onset of libido is potent and raw. I've never once felt this eager for a fucking cock. We take our time gliding through the yard as not to attract attention, but fuck, my insides are quaking with anticipation, and my pussy is fucking leaking.

We get to the gazebo, and I thank God the walls are solid, with only one entrance to watch. Doable. I'm hiking up my skirt as Zeke chuckles, and his zipper releasing is the only sound I care about.

I bend forward and plant my hands on the bench. "Quick and fast, Mr. Boudreaux."

His fingers run along my thong, and he growls when he finds how wet I am.

"Bebelle?" His voice is dark with promises of pain.

"I don't know." I shake my head. "I need you now, though."

He pulls my thong to the side, and I feel his wide, thick head press against my entrance. Then he's slowly pushing inside, and I can feel every cool ripple of his piercings. I'm being stretched, and the slight sting of pain makes me moan.

"Shh," he says as he grips my hips and bottoms out inside of me. "We don't want anyone to hear us." My heart ramps up with the fear of getting caught, but my pussy clamps down onto him with the same prospect. "Fuck," he grunts as he slaps my ass and pulls back out. "This pussy ..." he slams back in, making me jolt forward, "wants my cock to really..." pulls back out, my juices leak down my thighs, "... fucking punish her." His thrusts become harder.

"Please, Zeke." I don't know what I'm begging for, but I need this release like I need water to fucking survive.

"Hold on, quick and fast you said, right?"

I don't get the chance to answer as he pumps inside of me, his piercings hitting all the best places. I think it should be fucking mandatory for every girl to find at least one man with a fucking Jacob's Ladder to come on once in her life. There is no other feeling like it.

"Come for me," he growls, and slaps my ass once again.

With the sting of his slap, my walls tighten, and the force of my orgasm steals my breath. I can feel my pussy leaking around him, my insides are rippling, and my mouth is wide open in a silent scream. His onslaught continues as he chases his own orgasm while muttering behind me.

I see fucking stars as I crest, and then I'm nearly blacking out as my body tries to come back down from the high. He pulls out of me and lets his cum spray the floor under us. Right, no condom, and I'm due for my next shot soon.

"You definitely need that bathroom break." He chuckles as he puts my thong back into place.

I haven't moved, and my ass is still bent over as I try to regulate my heartbeat. I can feel the mess on my thighs, and I'm just grateful I chose black for tonight.

Finally, I stand and let the skirt fall back into place. My phone vibrates from my clutch on the seat, and I instantly know it's Caine.

"We've been gone a smidge too long." Zeke laughs as his phone chimes. He finishes doing himself up and pulls the phone from his pocket. "Sorry, we'll be in soon."

I hear a deep, growling voice on the other end, and smile at my correct assumption of who it was.

He hangs up with a grin and throws me a wink. "Someone's slightly jealous."

I bite into my lower lip and cringe. I don't want any of them to feel left out or neglected.

"Bebelle." He grabs my chin. "I'm kidding, and he knows the wait is worth it." He leans in and kisses me softly.

We hurry back inside, and I find a bathroom to clean up in. My panties are a fucking write off, but they'll have to do for the rest of the night.

We get back to the table, and my chest to my cheeks turn scarlet as everyone watches us approach. Cooper is the first to laugh, his dimples so deep, and his eyes squeezed shut.

"Sha, you look delectable," he continues to laugh.

"You didn't even finish your first glass of champagne," Kimmy pouts, and sways a bit with a burp.

"And you have had enough," Henry scolds her with an adoring look.

"Yeah, well, once the food gets here, I'll be able to have some more," she answers petulantly, and I laugh at her antics.

Zeke and I sit together, with Cooper on my right. Caine is across from me, shooting lustful looks, and I nearly moan when my pussy clenches. What the fuck is wrong with me?

I grab my glass of champagne and tip the contents back

in one gulp.

"Yes, girl!" Kimmy squeals and raises her hand. "Another round."

"Not until you eat." Henry lowers her hand with a chuckle.

"Fine." She grins. "At least get Kailey another one so she can catch up."

Caine raises his hand, his eyes still on me as a server rushes forward.

"Another champagne for the lady." He nods at me, but his eyes haven't left mine.

Am I in heat? Does this happen to humans? I avert my gaze and watch as the servers bring out the salad entrees. I need a fucking distraction right now.

The food is delectable. I've cleaned off every plate placed in front of me, and I've even dipped into Cooper's dessert.

"Watching you moan over that cheesecake is giving me ideas," he mutters, and my thighs clench.

I finish my second flute of champagne and notice everyone getting up to mingle or dance.

"Eyes on Cameron and his wife," Zeke mutters, and Caine gives an acknowledging nod.

"Boo!" Kimmy yells. "Let's go shake our bootays!"

She's so drunk.

"Okay." I smile and watch as Cooper stands to follow us.

Zeke gets up and heads in the opposite direction, while Caine remains at the table with Henry. He leans back in the chair, his legs spreading wide, and shoots me a wink when he catches me gawking.

I want between his legs.

I give myself a shake as Kimmy grabs my hand, and we end up in the middle of the dance floor. They aren't playing any popular music. It's a string band for fuck's sake, but Kimmy dances to it as I sway on the spot.

"You smell like citrus and sex," Cooper groans just behind me, and my almost dried panties are getting wet again. "I don't know how to explain what that scent does to a man."

He steps into my back, pressing himself into my ass. He's so fucking hard, and my body quivers with need.

"I don't know what's wrong with me," I tell him quietly. "It's like I can't turn it off."

"Maybe it's because we were apart, and now your body wants what it's been missing."

I turn around so we are face-to-face, our bodies pressed together, and his breath fanning over my skin.

"It's not just my body, Cooper. I've missed you too," I whisper as he gathers me up in his arms and twirls me out onto the dance floor.

The music has slowed down, and I see Henry pulling Kimmy into his arms as well. Cooper's steps are confident and strong as he leads us into a traditional waltz. I mean, they should be. I taught them all how to dance when we were younger.

People are watching us, and Cooper is eating up the attention as he twirls me around. This is his element, stealing the spotlight, and making himself seen.

His sure steps and straight posture have me biting my lip and staring into his eyes.

"Is it my turn to take you somewhere private now?" His voice rumbles, and the hand resting on my lower back slips down over my ass.

I nod and look around to see if anyone is paying attention to us. Cooper grabs my chin and pulls my eyes back to his.

"Don't worry, we have everything covered," he assures me.

I know they do. I know they would never let me be in any kind of danger, and right now, my hormones aren't letting me worry anyway.

He takes my hand and pulls me toward the bathroom I used after my time with Zeke. I know it's big enough, and the great thing is, it's a single occupancy only, with a large settee in the center.

Cooper's strides are long as he leads the way, both of us clouded by lust, and both of us about ready to rip our clothes off.

desecrated ESSENCE

BRODY

desecrated ESSENCE

THIRTY-SIX

What the fuck is Kimmy doing? Having a seizure? I watch as the blonde tries to dance to a string fucking band. *Jesus.*

The best thing about a masked anything is: blending into a room is a sure thing. The worst thing is so does everyone else. I have picked out the Ballon brothers since they surround themselves with security, and blending in was never something they were good at.

Kailey and my brothers are here, and they all look groomed and blended. Except for Kailey, she couldn't blend if she tried. Every man in the room has their eye on her, and I'd be lying if I said it didn't bother me. I'd also be lying if I said I didn't follow her and Zeke to that gazebo. That pierced dick of his really had her worked up from what I could hear.

Now, it looks like Cooper's turn to take Kailey for a ride. The bitch really hops from dick to dick, and that makes my blood boil. Fuck, maybe I'll get my chance later too.

Cameron makes a beeline for the bar, and I smirk, knowing he can't go too long without a drink… Those alcoholic tremors would give him away. He is the cruelest of the Ballon brothers, and I believe it's because he's the most useless. With no talent to boast of, Cameron has always lived off his father, clutching tight to his coattails his whole life. Now, he has to pull on the big boy pants and figure out how to control his wayward brothers.

Oh, not to mention, he has to figure out how to find me and bring me in for torture. I know I make it sound trivial, but really it is. I'm not afraid of torture, and I couldn't care less who's out to kill me. What I care about is putting my brothers in danger, and I guess her too.

Speaking of, I watch as they slyly round a corner and head for one of the many bathrooms in this mansion. There's not much going on right now, and I wouldn't mind watching yet another one of my brothers plow their girlfriend.

I lay my still full glass of champagne on the grand piano and head off in the direction they went. Both of them are idiots in lust, barely taking in their surroundings, and I convince myself I'm doing this to ensure their safety.

I get to the bathroom door and press my ear to the wood. The good thing about older homes is things were made right back then. Hardwood solid doors, hardwood solid floors, and walls coated in lead paint. The bad thing? Locks. All of the locks in this house can be easily picked open, and I tell myself again, I'm doing it to ensure they're safe.

I quickly but quietly unlock the door, and slowly open it to peer around inside the bathroom. I hear them, but I don't see them as I step inside and close the door behind me.

"I want you in my mouth," Kailey moans, and I mock gag.

This wanton whore sounds like she's been deprived of cock, which we all know isn't true. This bathroom is a large over-the-top show of wealth. The first room has a vanity with a large cushion chair and twinkling bulbs around the mirror. The next room has an ancient looking clawfoot tub and a single toilet sitting in the center… Slightly odd placement. The last room has a curtain covering the entrance, and this is where I hear them.

I stand to the side of the curtain, and drag it open, just a few inches. I immediately see Kailey on her knees, and Cooper with his head tossed back as she tries her best to swallow him whole. The slurping noises she makes has me cringing and growing hard simultaneously. I enjoy a good gag over a slurp, but hey, I'll take what I can get at this point.

He yanks her up by her biceps and devours her mouth, their tongues sloppily slurping, licking, and sucking. Gross. My cock jerks in my pants, and Monster caresses the inside of my chest. He also likes to watch, especially when it's Kailey. He'd just rather it be us.

She straddles his lap as she pushes him down to the small sofa. We hate this. We can't see a damn thing with her skirt in the way, and the tit he's latching onto is facing away from us.

Cooper's hand moves her skirt, and we finally get a good view of her ass as he moves her thong to the side. But it flicks back into place just as he guides her onto his cock. We growl in frustration as she rides him, but we can't see a fucking thing.

We imagine storming into the room, startling them both as we rip her dress off, push them both down, and ram into her tight asshole. Her screams of pain would ripple over us and heat our insides. We'd pound into her ass so hard; Cooper would feel the assault from inside her pussy, and the three of us would come together.

I shake my head, effectively dousing my fantasy, and watch

as Cooper slams up into Kailey, their wet skin slapping. She's getting louder, and he's grunting like a fucking pig. Suddenly, her head is tossing right and left as her body shakes with an orgasm. Cooper looks like the cat that got the cream as he watches her come with a smug smirk.

This is a little boring. I let the curtain slide back into place as I turn on my heel. I better not have missed too much for this subpar performance. I wonder if she misses my cock forcing its way inside her as she fights to get away… And now I'm hard again. I slip out of the bathroom locking it behind me, because there's no reason to cause a scene, and head back to the bar.

Sure enough, Cameron is still right where I left him, only now he's more boisterous as he talks about business with a few others. I do a quick scan of the room and find Zeke leaning against a far wall, giving him the perfect view of both Cameron and the hallway to the bathroom. I wonder how he really feels knowing his girlfriend is getting plowed by his brother.

Caine is sitting at the table with Henry and Kailey's annoying sidekick, Kimmy. Her voice and the hard pronounced country twang, makes me think I would kill her within a few days of dating her. To each their own.

The bartender makes her way to me as her eyes twinkle with attraction, and I roll mine at her obvious display. How the fuck can you see anything behind this mask?

"What can I get you, handsome?" she coos.

"Bottle of water," I answer shortly.

"Really?" Her brow lifts with what I imagine she thinks is a hot smirk on her face.

"Did I stutter?" I growl.

I watch as her spine straightens, and her eyes widen. She finally catches on that I'm not interested in her appeal and struts off to get the water.

"Chicks these days," a guy to my right chuckles. "What happened to being demure and waiting on a man's interest?"

"They were given the right to vote?"

The guy lets loose a loud laugh and pats my back with his hand. I breathe through the instincts to snap his neck and snatch the bottle of water out of the bartender's hand.

I turn away from him and the bar to head back over near the piano. It's in the center of the room and people constantly move around it in conversation. So not only do I see everyone, but I can also hear snippets of conversations too.

I watch Kailey and Cooper finally make their way back to the table, still straightening their clothing. I smirk when I see the dark look come over Caine's face.

They don't know how stupid they look for this girl. A girl with bright hazel eyes and lips like velvet.

KAILEY HIMARI

THIRTY-SEVEN

Cooper and I just christened that bathroom, and I am once again feeling sated. Caine keeps throwing me dark looks, looks that curl my toes and makes me want to beg for forgiveness. Not that he's making me feel like I did anything wrong, just that I haven't done it with him.

I don't know that I could ever fuck Caine in public. He has a way of pulling the loudest screams from me, all while inflicting the most delicious pain. Doesn't mean I wouldn't try it out, just that tonight's outing may not be the best place to test it. Besides, I am becoming paranoid that people are watching us, and I know I felt eyes on me in that bathroom.

"Kailey," Kimmy calls out. "Your mask is all flippy-doo."

"What?" I touch the mask.

"All wonky."

Jesus Christ.

Caine snorts, and Cooper chuckles as he straightens out the mask on my face.

"We've got eyes," Zeke mutters, and I begin to turn my head to see who's watching.

"Nuh uh, sha." Cooper holds my face still.

I guess Kimmy calling out my name attracted the people who were looking for us, and now our plan to just blend in is over.

"We should leave." My heart drops into my belly with fear.

"We can't leave yet," Caine says. "There's something going down here tonight."

"What if that something is us?" I grit out between my teeth.

"It's not." Zeke shakes his head. "Trust me."

I do, and that's the only reason I take my seat again. Another flute of champagne lands in front of me, and I have it to my mouth in seconds.

"Take it easy, ma petite." Caine smirks.

The way he looks at me always riles me up, and right now, my pussy is singing with an ache from being fucked hard … twice, but that doesn't stop my belly from swirling with heat and my thighs clenching with need.

Caine gets up from his seat and scoots Cooper down a few. Once he sits beside me, his hand curls around my thigh and his mouth lands at my ear.

"I can't fuck you here because you can't keep your pretty little mouth shut when I do." *See?* "But that doesn't mean you can't suck my dick."

Heat like molten metal settles between my legs as I think about Caine shoving that monster cock down my throat. I swallow audibly, and he chuckles.

"Tell me, ma petite. How bad do you want to swallow my cum?"

So bad.

"What are y'all talking about?" Kimmy calls across the table, her words slurring. "Henry, I want to go to Kailey."

I can't really handle a drunk Kimmy at the moment because I am trying really hard not to jump Caine and keep my cool while people plan our deaths.

I think of Brody in that second, and hope he's safe somewhere, even though he doesn't deserve my worry. I don't want him to die, though. Not unless it's me killing him for being the asshole he is. Then there's Oliver, my first to show me that love was something precious, and I worry about him too.

"Kailey is looking tired," Henry placates Kimmy. "Maybe we should get you home too."

"I'm not tired," she says through an enormous yawn that takes over her face.

We all chuckle as her head hits his shoulder and her eyes slowly drop close.

"Ten... Nine... Eight..." people begin to count down, and we all stand up out of our seats.

Oh!" Kimmy squeals, wrapping her arms around Henry's neck. "Let's go home and fuck."

Well then.

"Three... Two..."

Caine's mouth latches onto mine, and I hear cheers

all around me. When we break apart, I have Cooper's mouth opening around mine, and we indulge ourselves in the blissful contact. Then he's wrenched away, and Zeke is there, grabbing my face between his hands.

"I love you," he whispers, and I gasp at his confession.

He takes that opportunity to ravish my mouth, showing me just how much he really loves me. When we break apart, I feel the tears running down my cheeks.

"I love you too," I whisper.

"Boo!" Kimmy is next, throwing her arms around me and burying her face in my neck. "I love you."

"I love you too, Kimmy." I wrap my arms around my best friend.

"Happy New Year, Kailey," Henry says from behind her with a smile.

"You, too." I grin at him.

"Okay, buttercup." He pulls Kimmy off of me. "Ready to go home?"

"I am ready to climb you like a tall glass of water."

"Huh?" Caine looks at me, and I snort into my hand.

"Maybe she's dehydrated?" Cooper suggests, and we laugh as Henry takes her outside.

I turn my head and look toward the grand piano, stifling a yawn behind my hand. That's when I see him. I would know him anywhere. His body, and those eyes, will always be etched into my very soul.

He sees me and grins as he turns around, walking out the back door.

"He's here," I say to whoever is at my side, my eyes never leaving his retreating back.

"Who's here?" Caine asks.

"Brody!" I yell and dart after him.

Maybe it was the three flutes of champagne, or maybe in that moment I was just so desperate to be near him, I forgot to be cautious and screamed his name.

"Kailey." I hear Caine's harsh whisper, but I ignore him and chase after the boy who obliterated my heart.

I rush out the backdoor and almost barrel into Brody's back. He's still, too still, and his hands are raised above his head. The others storm out behind me but stop as soon as they see Brody.

"Kails." His voice is like water on a parched throat. "Do not move a fucking inch. Think you can listen to me just this once?"

"What's going on Brody?" I ask him.

When he doesn't answer, I look around him and see an overweight man, his mask pushed up on top of his head. He looks in his forties, but it's the eyes that cause me pause. They are the exact same shade of sterling silver that belong to another man who holds a piece of my heart.

"Cameron Ballon," Brody calls out, and the man lifts his eyes back up to Brody's. "I'm who you're looking for, right?"

"Who is she?" Cameron calls out, and I shudder at the sound of his voice. Nothing like Oliver's.

"She's nothing, just a little twit who can't let go of my dick." This asshole.

"Fuck you." I kick at his ankle.

"Will you three do your jobs and take the bitch inside?" Brody growls under his breath. "Go fuck her somewhere else."

I knew it! He was watching us.

"She's a pretty thing." This Cameron man is giving me the creeps. "I think she might be more important to you than you're saying."

"Oh, yeah?" Brody sneers, and I watch as he steps aside, completely exposing me. "Kill her."

"What?' I growl at him.

Nobody moves as Cameron swings his gun and points it at me. His fat, sweating face puffs up into a cruel smile. "You sure?" he asks Brody.

"I told you I don't care about her. Use her as a target for all I care."

The small pieces of my heart that still held out hope for the damaged boy I once loved burns into nothing. He let go of me a long time ago.

I watch as Cameron's shooter finger presses into the trigger, and I feel someone behind me grabbing my dress. I clamp my eyes shut and wait for the shot. This man has it out for Brody, and if there's any chance he thinks Brody is lying, then he'll use it.

"Kailey-Himari Richard," Caine growls, and I hear Cameron hum.

"This is Charles Richard's daughter." He chuckles. "I will kill her as payback for her father reneging on his deal."

"Go ahead," Brody taunts.

I hear the shot, but my mind takes a while to process what's happening and why my face is smeared into the earth.

Not something I ever wanted to happen to me again. The body on my back is like lead, and I try to wiggle out so I can breathe.

"Stop moving," Caine grunts.

"She's lucky she has a couple bodyguards, huh?" Cameron chuckles. "He was all too happy to take a shot for her."

"Caine!" I shrill.

"I'm fine. The fucker missed." He gets up, and I see Zeke and Cooper have moved into position in front of us.

"Will you fucking take her inside?" Brody growls under his breath. The asshole is going to get a punch in the face.

As soon as Caine is off of me, I see red, and Brody's head turns in slow motion just as I snarl.

I push between Cooper and Zeke, just trying to get to him when he jumps out in front of the three of us. His eyes widen, and I hear a bang, followed closely by another. Zeke yells and reaches out to Brody as Cooper turns and grabs me around the waist.

I watch Caine jump to his feet and run to where Zeke is crouched on the ground.

No.

Where is he? Did he just take a bullet for me?

Please, no.

I shove Cooper's arms off me and run forward, tripping on my shoes. I fall into Caine and shove him away.

No.

Zeke is saying something as he rocks back and forth, and it feels like it's taking my body forever to get to him.

Please, no.

I fall to my knees and crawl toward him as he lies still on the ground.

"Just keep your eyes open, okay?" I hear Zeke moan.

No ... no.

"Brody?" My voice is small and meek. He would hate it and tell me I sound stupid.

His head turns slowly as I crawl the rest of the way to him. He's pale and there's a small trickle of blood escaping his mouth.

God, no... I can't lose him.

"Kails..." His voice is barely a whisper, and I suck back a sob threatening to push its way out. He would hate that even more. "I..."

"Get his jacket off." *Oliver?*

I look up and see my fourth boyfriend rushing over and kneeling beside Brody. Did he shoot him?

"Where was he hit?" Oliver rips Brody's jacket open, and I gasp when I see his white shirt saturated in red.

No.

Oliver rips that shirt open, and I scream when I see the blood pooling around a hole in the center of his chest. Oliver whips his sweater off and pushes it down on top of Brody's chest.

Cooper tries to grab me, but Brody's head is still facing me and his mouth is moving.

I lean my ear down over his mouth.

"Kails..." He sounds so small, so weak. "Don't ... hate me ... any less."

"I won't." I cry. I love him. No matter what, I will always love the boy with icy blue eyes who stepped in front of a bullet meant for me.

"Be … vibrant and … free."

"No, Brody. No!" I scream. "Don't you dare leave me! Don't you even dare!" I grab his face as his head lolls.

"Kail." Oliver's voice penetrates my wails. "I need to help him. Go with the others."

"I'm not leaving," Zeke moans as he cries for his brother, his closest friend.

The sirens start in the background, a slow, low wail, and Caine bends down to lift me up.

"No!" I scream.

"Please." Caine's voice trembles. "Please let us get you out of here. He would want that."

"No! I'm not leaving him again!" I scream.

Caine picks me up off my feet, and I kick out as I struggle to get away. I see Cooper grabbing Zeke, and we all head toward the front. I look back one last time to see Oliver pumping into Brody's chest, and Cameron Ballon's body sprawled out with a single shot between his eyes.

"No!" I scream, reaching my hand out. "No!"

God, please, no.

KAILEY HIMARI

THIRTY-EIGHT

6 months later...

The stage is decorated in J.F. Kennedy Prep's colors, gold and blue. The podium stands dead center stage, and the teacher's chairs are in one row. I squirm in my seat as sweat slides down my tailbone and into my pants.

It's a fucking scorcher today, and of course, our graduation falls on it. I want to be home in my sweats, eating a gallon of ice cream and watching a bad soap opera. Cooper leans over and runs his tongue up my neck, making me shiver at the touch.

"You look so fucking sexy, sha," he croons.

"Don't get her any squirmier than she already is," Caine growls and his voice has me biting my lip.

I have been completely insatiable these last few months, like I can't get enough of my men's dicks, and most days, I feel like my house is a sex den.

"Good evening, J.F. Kennedy's graduating class." Oliver's voice rings clear over the mic, and my panties soak at the sound.

"Oh, fuck." Zeke leans over Caine and looks into my face. "Someone's got it bad for Teacher."

Kimmy turns in her seat in front of us to throw me a wink and a giggle.

He's damn right I do. Zeke has also grown on me quite a bit in the last six months, and just fit into the fold like he was always meant to be there. He's been seeing his therapist for the cutting and has definitely brought his life back to his own. He hasn't cut a single time since saying goodbye to his mother for good. That stress is gone, and he's a lighter, happier person.

"You keep looking like that, and I will take you back to our bathroom," Caine grumbles.

Ah, yes… Our bathroom. The one he made me suck his dick in at the beginning of the year. *Everything* has changed since then.

"I will begin to call the graduates up in alphabetical order." Our principal takes over from Oliver, and he shoots me a wink from the stage. I'm totally riding his cock later.

The principal calls out the names. The first to go up is Kimmy. She looks radiant and happy. Then we hear Ezekiel Boudreaux. We all jump to our feet and cheer as Zeke rises and saunters up to the stage. He is sex on two legs, and I am one lucky girl to have him. He flips everyone the bird, and we all laugh.

Before long, Cooper Fontenot is called out, and the whole graduating class erupts into riotous cheering. Cooper, star quarterback of J.F. Kennedy Prep, has won a full scholarship to Tulane and will join their football team in the fall.

Next up is Caine Leblanc, and I am the only one left in my seat screaming as he gets up and smashes his lips to mine. The guys on the stage catcall, and I can feel the furious blush that steals up my chest and face.

Caine commands every room—or in this case, the football field—whenever he enters it. He claims anything he fucking wants, regardless of anyone's feelings, and I love him so fucking much.

"Kailey-Himari Richard," the principal calls out, and I stand to my guys causing a ruckus on stage. I don't have any family here for me today, but I know a few up in heaven watching over me.

"She's gotten so fat," Connie snickers as I walk by her, and I roll my eyes.

Connie took over as the queen hound when Georgina was declared a runaway and forgotten about. Casey and Faith follow her around just like they did with Georgie, never, ever making it on their own.

I take the five stairs up to the stage and stop in front of his picture. This whole ceremony is in memory of him, the boy who once stole my heart and then crushed it as he reveled in my pain. Brody Landry, my best friend and worst enemy.

I kiss my fingers and run it along his cheek.

I love you.

Then I collect my diploma, shake hands with Oliver, and stand between my guys as they hug me to them. My heart is full of the family I made, and I know Mama is proud of the survivor I've become.

There will always be a dark part of my heart reserved just for him, for the boy who I loved to hate, and in return, craved my hatred. Brody Landry.

Oliver tried to save him that night, but he couldn't. The bullet from Cameron's gun was fatal, and Brody died as I was reaching my hand out, screaming for him. Oliver made the quick decision to remove his body before the police got there, and later claimed to be the one to kill Brody, effectively cutting out his family.

Brody's body was disposed of in the same fashion as Papa's. The only difference was we had a private ceremony for Brody in my backyard. It was a clear, beautiful day, and the sun shone down between the vines of the purple Wisteria like fingers to touch our faces. I want to believe it was him, that he was finally at rest, and his battle here on Earth's plane was ultimately over.

I was pissed at Oliver for a few months, but I began to understand why he did what he did. He didn't want his family to claim a Landry kill because they would then gain that power and mow over the other families. Those other families are now my guys. They have taken over during the Ballon's uncertain time of losing their patriarch and oldest son. The Ballons will never regain their footing.

Now my four guys run New Orleans, and I support them completely. My future plans are uncertain right now, but at least I know *they* are my future, regardless of what I do.

And then one day, I will reunite with *him* too.

"I am starving!" I exclaim as soon as I step foot in the house.

Cooper's arms wrap around my waist from behind and

his mouth presses into my neck.

"What do you want?" he asks, his breath fanning my cheek and his body pressing into mine.

"Yeah, bebelle." Zeke steps up in front of me. "What do you want?"

"She said she was hungry, not horny." Caine comes inside and growls.

"Actually…" I stare into Zeke's eyes and bite my lip.

Caine grabs my hand and pulls me out from between them. "Eat first," he says as he leads me into the kitchen. I *am* horny.

"Or we can do both like last time," Cooper calls out, and I gasp at the memory.

Ice cream, whipped cream, and chocolate sauce. Three of us writhing on the bed, the sheets soiled beyond saving, and my screams shattering the night's silence.

"Yeah, we could do that since I missed out on it last time," Zeke adds.

Cooper, Caine, and Zeke don't mind doubling down—or tripling down, sometimes—with me. They don't really cross swords though, and that's okay because I really like their undivided attention on me. Oliver is the one who would rather not share, and I'm okay with that too. He's really opened up, and I call him Mr. Kink on occasions, although lately he's been more cautious.

Caine drops a plate with a sandwich on it in front of me, and my mouth salivates when I see it's my favorite. Tomato with pickles and cheese.

I hear the front door open and shut, then Oliver strides into the kitchen. He leans over and kisses my cheek, then takes a seat beside me.

"This sandwich again?" he teases.

I take a bite of the sandwich and close my eyes on a moan. *So good.*

"Jesus," he groans, and I open my eyes to see him readjusting himself in his slacks.

"Yeah," Caine mutters and licks his lips.

"Sorry." I grin ruefully.

"They did a good job for the dedication today," Cooper says as he stands in the kitchen's entryway.

"Took some convincing." Oliver shakes his head. "There hasn't been a body found and his parents refuse to declare him dead."

Brody's parents aren't giving in to the story Oliver provided, and Brody's father especially, is the biggest naysayer.

I drop the sandwich back on the plate, my appetite gone, and my chest once again feeling heavy.

"Give me a minute," I tell everyone as I get up out of my seat.

I walk out into the backyard and head straight for the pruned Wisteria. It no longer engulfs the gazebo, and I train my eyes on the opening, praying he'll just come out laughing at us for thinking he was dead.

No matter how cruel he was, or what he put me through, I'm having a hard time letting him go, and it just feels like we have too much unfinished business. I lift my hand to my right breast, exactly where the scars of his initials still brand my skin and look to the sky.

I hate you much less now, Brody Landry.

desecrated ESSENCE

EPILOGUE

The house looks dark from across the street. Like a large looming structure waiting for an innocent soul to pass its gate and suck them dry. I cross the street and hop the fence into the backyard. Things change, but some things will always remain the same.

The purple vines sway in the slight breeze and the gazebo once again sits proud and prominent. I'm glad she took the time to clean it up. Her mother would be happy to see it this way.

I look up to the second-story balcony and listen closely. There's no noise, not even a creak, and I second guess what the fuck I'm doing and why I'm here. If I'm caught, everything is over. I would kiss my life goodbye, and all of theirs.

I'm here though, and I couldn't stay away, not when my very own *what could have been* is in there.

I climb the fence and pull myself up onto the balcony, then freeze. I listen closely and when I still don't hear a single sound, I press my hand to the window. Would Zeke have fixed it knowing it's a weak point in his security?

If he didn't, I can get in, but I will be fucking pissed that he put her at risk like that. I push up a bit on the window and curse under my breath as it moves. Bastard. If anything, it glides even smoother now, absolutely no noise as it drags along the track and stops at the top.

I pull the sheer fabric of the curtain aside and peer into the darkened room. Nothing moves, no sounds, and the house remains completely still. I know they are all home… I watched them come in here and settle in for the night. Do they sleep that dead to the world? In this unsecured house?

I pull myself inside and, again, pause as I wait. Nothing. I exhale my breath and move around the room. They changed it, just like I thought they would, and it looks great for the purpose it's serving.

I touch the chair in the corner, set up beside a bookcase, and I bend down to read some titles. The Very Hungry Caterpillar by Eric Carle, many Dr. Seuss books, and an old worn copy of Winnie the Pooh by A.A. Milne. I remember that one when we were kids, and how often Sara would read it to us.

There are large, plush teddy bears around the room, and pictures line the walls. I want to look at them all, but I don't have any time to spare. It's the lettering over the crib that makes me still in my tracks as I try to catch my breath.

Broderick.

Walking to this crib is the longest trip I've ever made, even though it's just a few steps. I have never had my heart beat like this. I have never felt such fear, and for the first time in my life, I'm alive. I see a slight movement in the crib, a little fist shoots up, and the cloth on the arm is blue.

When I get to the crib, I will myself to relax. This feels

like the one and only moment in life I was meant to live for. The only reason I'm still here walking this Earth is for the little human in this crib. I open my eyes and bend to look in.

So small, so delicate, and so much like Kailey. His skin is paler, but his little pouty mouth and slightly upturned eyes are hers. He has dark brown hair on his head and it's long, thick, curly at the ends. I run my hand through my hair as it flops down my forehead and curls at the ends. My heart jumps again. She has a small, red pouch tied to the crib over his head. A Gris-Gris.

I reach in and run my fingers over the soft skin on his cheek, imprinting the feel in my brain. I want to relive this moment when I'm alone again. His mouth turns up into an almost cruel looking grin in his sleep, and I stand still watching until it fades away.

Could it be?

Then, as if he senses me, his eyes open slowly and look up into my face curiously. His eyes. I cover my mouth with my hand to cover the startled noise. Those eyes.

Icy blue, like the arctic snow reflecting the sky. Those eyes stare straight into my soul.

My eyes.

Those eyes scan over my face, and his brows come together slightly, confused about who I am. Is he old enough to know I'm a stranger? Am I truly a stranger, though?

He makes a little noise and grins again.

"Shh." I put my finger to my mouth and watch as his little hand shoots up.

I touch his fist, and his little fingers latch around one of mine like a vise. Then, amazingly, I watch as he turns a bit and snuggles into his blanket, still gripping my finger. Just like that, he's back to sleep, and I know I've spent too much time here.

I pull my finger away and creep back to the window, casting one more look over my shoulder. It'll be the last one for a very long time. Then I'm back out of the window, closing it shut, and my feet back down on solid ground.

"That wasn't too smart," The Teacher says from behind me.

I knew it was too easy. I turn and look at Oliver, a grin coming over his face.

"I guess not. You should probably fix that window," I tell him.

"Clearly." He nods. "Find what you're looking for?"

"Yeah."

"Now you have to forget it, Landry," he growls and steps closer.

"I can't do that." I shake my head.

"I helped you live, gave you a life away from this and did everything you asked of me," he grits out, anger lining his features.

"I know. That was the plan, Oliver." I point up to that second-story window. "But that changes everything." He drops his head to his chest and exhales. He has to know that the child up there changes our deal. "I can't be here with him right now, I know that," I tell him, then watch as his head snaps up. "I need you to raise him tough. Tougher than you and me."

His eyes narrow and his brow rises.

"Because I will be back one day, not soon, but I will be back, and I need him tough."

Oliver begrudgingly nods.

"He's my son, and one day… He'll know his real father." Then I turn my back on him and the most important thing in the world.

My very own bolt of lightning.

For all book updates and social platforms, check out my website

ABOUT THE AUTHOR

C.A. Rene lives in Toronto, Canada with her family, where most of the year varies from chilly to frigid. Most days you'll find her wrapped in her many blankets in bed while reading or writing her next dark, twisted story.

Her stories boast of inclusivity and refusal to be conformed in any small box. Writing across genres is a hobby and drinking wine is a must... Or coffee ... with a splash of Baileys.

ALSO BY CA RENE

THE WHITSBOROUGH CHRONICLES
Through the Pain
Into Darkness
Finding the Light
To Redemption

THE WHITSBOROUGH PROGENIES
Ivy's Venom
Carmelo's Malice
Saxon's Distortion
Gabriel's Deception

DESECRATED DUET
Desecrated Flesh
Desecrated Essence

THE REAPED SERIES
The Reaper Incarnate
Hunting the Reaper
Claiming the Reaper

HAIL MARY DUET
Blue 42
Red Zone

SACRIFICIAL LAMBS
Sing Me a Song
Song of Tenebrae
A Verse for Caelum
A Harmony of Procellarum

STEEL DRAGONS MC
Dragon Slayer
Dragon Strife
Dragon Slayer

HELL'S MARCH MC
Hell's Viper

THE PHANTOM CHASERS
Bedlams Playground
Silent Night Theme Park

STANDALONES
Fighting the Tide
Festum Mors
Genesis